Merging 1

Dark Codes

Marissa Farrar

Chapter One

I paced the floor of the medical level, waiting for what I hoped would be Alex declaring Clay's clean bill of health.

"Quit stressing, love," Isaac said from beside me. "Clay's fine. This is just a formality so Devlin can sign him off as being fit to get back to work."

I chewed on my lower lip and glanced back toward the closed door. I could have been in there with them, but I figured Clay was entitled to some privacy. I shouldn't be overly worried. After all, Lorcan had been allowed to return shortly after he'd been shot, but time was ticking by, and every minute waiting felt like a minute wasted. Now that I'd officially been made a part of the team, I wanted us all together. Going out there with someone missing just felt wrong.

Besides, it was more important than ever that each of us was well enough to work. The man who'd killed my father now had the memory stick which gave the locations of each of these training bases across the country. The men who were trained there worked as undercover spies to take out people responsible for corruption in the country, and crooked men like Special Agent Lyle Hollan wanted to see them dead.

The atmosphere in the center had completely changed from when I'd first arrived. Where before there had been a relaxed congeniality, now the tension vibrated through the air, infecting everyone like bacteria. Perhaps that was why I was so anxious about Clay, even though he'd been sitting up in bed and talking the last time I'd seen him. The man who oversaw this base, Devlin, had assured us that we were the best protected out of all of the centers, as we were prepared for the pos-

1

sibility of Hollan attacking, but it still felt as though we were fish in a barrel down here. Devlin pointed out that we had cameras covering the surrounding area, and we'd know if anyone so much as looked in our direction in the wrong way, but that didn't help my nerves.

"I know," I replied, "but I can't shake the feeling that we're going to end up fighting for our lives at any moment."

"You know what Devlin said." Isaac glanced at me. "Hollan isn't going to come here. He knows this is our base, and that we're both going to be on a race to reach the other bases first. He'll be dividing men up and trying to hit as many as possible before we can get there to warn them."

"Which is why we need to get the hell out of here as soon as we can."

"Devlin's bringing us in transport. You have to trust him."

I nodded, hoping Isaac was right. I wanted to trust that Devlin was doing the right thing, but things had gotten so personal between me and Hollan while he'd been holding me captive that I couldn't shake the feeling he would try to come for me first.

My synesthesia had allowed me to memorize the five sets of coordinates that had been the information on the flash drive my dad had died trying to protect. That information should only ever have been in Devlin's hands, but now Hollan and his men had it, too.

We needed to warn the other bases that Hollan was on his way. The longer we waited, the more chance there was of Hollan reaching them before we did.

Isaac turned to face me and caught up my hand.

There was something about Isaac. He wasn't big and muscular like Kingsley, or sexy and easygoing like Clay, and he didn't even have Lorcan's dark broodiness, or Alex's prep-school, blond good looks. He was shorter than the others, freshly shaved, with neatly cut brown hair and green eyes, but he was serious, and had a kind of aura about him that others, myself included, paid attention to. Plus, that British accent, which he still had left over from his childhood, was sexy as hell.

"I know things haven't always been easy between us," he said. "But I just wanted you to know I'm pleased you're a part of our team."

His gaze bored into my face, and I felt my cheeks heat at his intensity.

The memory of how he'd held me in the cabin while he'd pushed his fingers inside me flashed into my head, and my blush deepened.

"Thanks, Isaac. I'm happy to be a part of it, too."

He moved in closer, so my breasts were an inch away from his chest, and only my t-shirt and the buttons of the blue shirt he wore separated our skin. He tilted his head slightly, in a way I knew was a habit of his when he was thinking of something, but that also made me think he was going to lean in and kiss me.

"I need you to do something for me, though." His voice was low and sexy. The sound made my heart beat faster. "The other guys care about you. You know that, don't you?"

I swallowed and nodded. "Yeah, I guess."

"They will literally lay down their lives for you."

"I'd do the same for them," I blurted, but he lifted his finger between us to tell me to be quiet.

"You're not understanding what I'm saying to you. I'm asking you not to do anything that's going to put one of them in a situation where they're going to have to put themselves in danger to get you out of a situation you've thrown yourself in the middle of. You're all about the numbers, Darcy. Remember your skills—the reason you've been added to the team—and try not to get yourself or anyone else killed."

His words stung, and I didn't like hearing them. I glanced away, my lips pressed together.

"Hey," he said, more softly. He reached out to touch my chin, bringing my gaze back to his. "I'm not saying this to upset you. I'm saying it because I want each one of us to come back alive, okay?"

"You think I'm a liability." I didn't phrase my words as a question.

"I think you haven't had the same training as the others, and you make rash, headstrong decisions. I'm not saying that's always a bad thing, but when you're a team member, things need to be done as a group."

I forced myself to hold his gaze. "Then you need to listen to me a little more, too." I fought my corner. "Don't just dismiss me because I'm a girl."

He shook his head. "I'd never do that."

"Good."

His fingers were still on my chin, the warmth of his skin flooding through mine. It was just the two of us in the corridor, and my breath caught, anticipating what might happen next. I'd spent time with each of the other guys—okay, I'd had sex of some kind with each of the other guys—but other than that one time when he'd pushed his fingers inside me in front of the others, Isaac and I hadn't spent any intimate time together. I didn't know why that was. Had he been keeping me at arm's length for a reason, or was it because he simply didn't like me in the way the others seemed to? Maybe he was less keen on the idea of sharing?

I had to admit, being shared between a group of hot guys wasn't how I'd expected my future relationships to go either, but this wasn't something any of us had planned. We'd just kind of fallen into it. In fact, we hadn't even really sat down and talked things out yet. Right now, I couldn't bring myself to think about a future and how this would work, assuming they even wanted to stay with me. Would they want to have other girlfriends as well? A stab of jealousy shot through me at the idea. How crazy, that I was happy for them to each share me, but the thought of another woman coming into the mix made me as green as moss.

I thought Isaac would drop his hand from my chin and step away, but I wasn't going to be the one to make the first move. Instead, he leaned in a little closer, his eyes never leaving mine. My pulse raced in anticipation, and lightly, oh so lightly, he brushed his lips to mine.

My eyes slipped shut, and I leaned into him, my body instantly surging with longing. How often did we want something even more when we felt like we couldn't have it? Isaac had always been kind of standoffish with me, and having him kiss me now, with no one else around, made my heart swell.

We moved in closer, our bodies pressing flush against each other. I'd gotten a look at Isaac's torso when I'd stabbed him back in the days of the cellar, and had seen the magnificent dragon tattoo on his back. I liked that about him—how he seemed so clean cut on the outside, while hiding something like that beneath the expensive shirts and suit jackets.

Our lips parted, and his tongue darted into my mouth, touching with mine. I pressed myself closer, my arms wrapping around his neck. He was only a little taller than I was, and already I could feel that he wanted me, the hard ridge of him pressing against my stomach. Where his hand had been lightly resting beneath my chin, it now slid around the back of my neck, his fingers knotting in my hair. His other hand slipped up the side of my body, seeking its way beneath my t-shirt and moving between us to cup my breasts over my bra. His fingers pinched the already hard nub of my nipple. I gasped at the forcefulness of his kiss, and my palms ached to touch his skin. I reached down to his sides, tugging the carefully tucked-in shirt out of his suit pants. Then my hands moved up inside his shirt, and I ran my fingers across the smooth skin of his back, my mind's eye picturing the design of the dragon beneath my palms.

He worked my breast free of the cup of my bra, and his thumb circled my bare nipple, making me groan. We were standing in the middle of the corridor, and though there weren't supposed to be cameras inside the building to monitor the everyday lives of those who lived here, I knew there was a chance we could be interrupted at any moment. I wanted to drag him back to the room that had become my bedroom and throw myself down on the bed for him to do whatever he wanted, but we were waiting for Alex and Clay, and I knew we had more pressing matters at hand. Sex was a way of escaping it all, however. It was the one time I found I was able to forget everything else that had happened, or stop worrying about the past or the future, and just live completely in the moment. I wanted to grab his hand and shove it down the front of my jeans, to feel his fingers inside me like I had that day at the cabin, with all the guys watching me climax, but a click came from the door, signaling it opening.

Isaac and I jumped apart, both of us flustered, quickly putting our clothes back together, like two teenagers caught making out by their parents.

Alex lifted his eyebrows and looked between us, a smirk on his face. Clay was close behind, fully dressed again in his usual jeans and t-shirt combo. It was good to see him looking like himself.

"We interrupting something?" Alex asked.

"Not at all." Isaac stood straighter. "We were just passing time while waiting for you."

"How's the patient looking, Doc?" I asked Alex, trying to hide the fact I'd been practically climbing Isaac only moments before.

Alex grinned over his shoulder at Clay. "He's good to go. No signs of any lasting effects from the knock to the head. Just try to make sure you don't make it a habit, okay?"

"I wasn't exactly looking for it," Clay pointed out.

"No," Isaac said, already back to his commanding self, "but you put yourself in a position of vulnerability. No more risks, okay?"

He glanced over to me as he said it, and I knew he was talking about me as well. Clay had been injured because he'd sacrificed himself for my freedom. Isaac was telling me not to put Clay in the position where he'd need to do something like that again. I hoped neither of us would need to.

Clay threw me a wink. "Since when do I ever take risks, right, sugar?"

I suppressed a smile.

Alex nodded at me. "And what about that hand of yours? How does it feel?"

"Okay. The swelling's gone down loads, and it's nowhere near as painful."

Alex held out his hand to me, and dutifully I placed the hand which had suffered from the dislocated fingers into his palm. He frowned down at it, gently turning my hand over, depressing my injury with a firm but gentle touch.

Finally, he smiled and released me. "Yeah, it does look better. You take care with it, though, okay? No trying to catch any balls with that hand."

I cocked an eyebrow at him. "I don't think we're going to play sports anywhere in our immediate future."

He chuckled. "You know what I mean."

A different voice called to us from the other end of the corridor. "Ah, good, I've found the rest of you."

We all turned to where Devlin had appeared. The man who led the base was older than the others, in his forties, with dark hair flecked with white at the temples. Like Isaac, he had an air of authority, and the way he was always smartly dressed also helped to convey his position of power.

"Kingsley and Lorcan are waiting for you in the control room," he continued, his deep blue eyes flicking between us, a slight frown causing the lines on his brow to deepen.

Lorcan had been given the job of doing an inventory of the weapons available in the base. Previously, other than the guns used for target practice, the men and boys living in the base weren't armed. That was another thing that had changed. Now anyone who could handle a gun had access to one. That wasn't saying we were all carrying, but instead distribution points had been set up on each level, so if the warning came through that we were under attack, anyone who could handle a weapon would be issued one. Some of the boys were still deemed to be too young—though they weren't happy about the situation—but anyone over the age of sixteen would be allowed to carry. We needed all the help we could get.

Kingsley was talking to the younger trainees, teaching them what to do if the base was attacked. These kids were too young to fight back, so they needed to hide and wait for the adults to deal with things. Kingsley taught coping mechanisms, ways to stay calm even if it felt like there was chaos all around them. I prayed it wouldn't come to that, but if it did, I hoped the boys would remember to stay out of the way and not try to do anything stupid. My aunt, Sarah, would also stay with them. I liked that they had a maternal figure around them now, and the boys all seemed to like her around, too. She wouldn't be fighting, so it made sense for her to stay with the boys to offer them comfort and reassurance should anything happen.

Devlin looked to Alex. "I assume Clay is fit to be back in the field?"

"Yeah, he seems to be firing on all cylinders, or at least as much as Clay ever is."

Clay punched him in the shoulder.

"Watch it, buddy," Alex warned.

"Be thankful it wasn't your face, otherwise you'd be the one back in the medical bay, and as a patient this time instead of the doctor."

The two of them were only messing around. I knew neither would want to see the other one hurt.

"That's enough, you two," Devlin said. "We've got work to do."

I was glad Devlin hadn't been the one to catch me and Isaac making out a moment before. I had no idea what the older man thought was going on between us all, but I doubted he'd know the full extent of it, or he might have been a little less ready to add me to the team. I knew my aunt had suspicions, and she and Devlin had gotten friendly over the last few days, but I hoped she wouldn't break my trust, yet again, by talking behind my back to Devlin about my private life.

We turned to walk toward the elevator to take us to the upper level, where the surveillance equipment, and I assumed weapons, were kept. Before we reached the elevator, Isaac's shoulder brushed mine.

"We'll finish this off later," he murmured in my ear, and a thrill raced through me.

I just hoped we'd get a later.

Chapter Two

Kingsley and Lorcan were waiting for us as the elevator doors opened and deposited us in the control room. Other men were around as well, men I'd now come to recognize and who had grown used to me in turn. They were the ones tasked with the general day-to-day running and security of the base, and they were certainly earning their pay now.

The other men faded into the background for me, however. My guys would always stand out brighter—the men who made my heart race and feel as though life was worth living again.

Kingsley smiled at me, his teeth white against the dark of his skin. He really was a striking man, and every time he caught my eye, my heart flipped. It was hard not to react to Kingsley. He was one of those men who got noticed constantly—all six feet something of him, with his deep voice and smooth manner.

Lorcan remained in the background. He looked even more dangerous than his dark hair and tattoos normally alluded to, but this time it was because he was surrounded by guns. Multiple cases lay open, displaying the weapons within. We weren't going to go into this without being prepared, and it looked to me like Devlin assumed we were going to need some serious firepower.

"How's the patient?" Kingsley asked.

Clay waved a hand. "Hey, I am here, you know. Everyone is welcome to speak to me directly."

Kingsley ignored him and continued to talk to Alex. "I assume he's fine."

Alex chuckled. "Yeah, and ready to go."

"Too damned right," Clay agreed, rubbing his hands together. "No way am I going to let that fucker abduct Darcy and then hit me around the head without me delivering some justice."

I lifted my eyebrows at him. "I have some justice of my own I want to send his way," I reminded Clay.

"Then we'll do it together, sugar. A regular ol' Bonnie and Clyde."

I frowned. "Weren't they the criminals?"

He laughed. "You know what I'm sayin.'"

Devlin stepped in. "Okay, enough of that. We need to focus. Transport will be here for you in an hour, and you need to be ready when it arrives."

Nerves tumbled in my stomach. I wanted to get out of here and start our mission—my first official mission, and possibly the most important I'd ever have—but the thought still made my mouth run dry. There was always the possibility things would go wrong, and, as always, the fear of losing one of the guys hung over me. I guessed it was something that would constantly haunt me now. We had dangerous jobs, and I'd lived most of my life with a father who'd also had a dangerous job. Trouble was, he hadn't come out of it alive, so my fears were perfectly rational.

"As you can see," Devlin continued, "we have plenty of weapons for you to take, together with ammo. I'd like to say I hope you won't need to use them, but you don't know what you're going to find. Remember the other bases don't yet know we have a way of contacting them either, so there's a chance they may be hostile until you're able to prove who you are."

"How are we going to do that?" Isaac interrupted.

"I'll give you ID and a code word. Ask to speak with whoever is running the show. They'll know the word. It's the one thing that allows us to coordinate in case of an emergency, or something bigger than one unit can handle."

"Such as multiple terrorist units infiltrating the government," Lorcan said.

Devlin nodded. "Or homegrown terrorists like Hollan. That man is dangerous, and not just on a personal level. He wants to manipulate government to make decisions that will benefit him financially—for the companies he's invested in. He'll happily create a situation which might end up with the United States declaring war on another country if it means lining his own pocket. And he's not the only one. That's why we exist, and the other bases like ours. When the people we trust to keep us and our country safe are as corrupt as our enemies, we're the only ones who can keep this country and its inhabitants safe. They may not realize it, but the lives of the American people lie in our hands."

Isaac gave a sharp nod. "We won't let you down."

"Let me take you through the equipment. We can't assume all the bases are underground, like this one. I'm not saying they won't be, but they're as likely to be in an industrial building, or hell, even disguised as offices. I'm not expecting them to be in the middle of any built-up areas, however. Questions would quickly be asked if suspicious looking people were seen coming in and out." He produced a piece of equipment and laid it out on the table. "These are thermal imaging goggles. As you know, even with the coordinates, the possible locations still cover large areas. If it looks like the base attached to those coordinates might have the same setup as this one, you can use the heat sensors to find it. With this many people and this much equipment underground, it will give off an obvious reading compared to the rest of the surrounding area.

"I've sent the aerial screen shots of each of the locations to your laptop, Isaac. I struggled with a couple of the locations due to cloud cover, but I've done what I can. I wish we could be more specific about the exact positions of the bases, but the coordinates would have had to have been multiple digits long to be that precise. What we've got should be close enough for you to figure it out, however. You've grown up in this place, and you know what to look for."

Isaac nodded. "We'll find them, and before Hollan does, too. That we already know how these bases operate is one big advantage we have over him."

I prayed Isaac was right, and we did have an advantage over Hollan. It gave me a little flicker of hope that everything would be all right.

"It makes sense for you to head to the closest base first. It's about five hundred miles from here, in an area outside of Atlanta."

Five. Zero. Zero. The numbers appeared in the space around my head.

The spark of hope I'd experience fizzled and died. Damn it. It would take us hours to get there, almost the whole day. I wondered how far all the other locations were if that was the closest. Of course I knew how big our country was, but I'd been holding on to the idea that they'd have been located in at least the same state so they could coordinate with each other.

"How much time have we got before we need to leave?" Isaac asked.

Devlin checked his watch. "We're down to forty minutes now, and I need you and all the gear above ground in that time, too."

I chewed on my lower lip. "Have I got time to go and say goodbye to my aunt?"

He nodded. "You're not to tell her anything about where you're going, though."

"I understand."

I didn't blame him for being cautious. After what my aunt had done, contacting Hollan behind our backs, I wouldn't have trusted her with this information either. But that didn't mean I didn't love her, and if anything happened to me, I'd at least want to know that we'd said a final farewell. I'd never had that with my dad. He'd been snatched from me so suddenly, and what followed had just been confusion and panic. He'd taken the time to tell me the numbers to unlock the memory stick, but hadn't told me how much he'd loved me, or that he was proud of me. I knew it was a necessary thing now, and my life would currently be on a whole other track if he hadn't, but that didn't prevent me from doing everything I could to make sure I never lost a loved one without saying goodbye again.

Leaving the guys still talking with Hollan, I got back into the elevator car and went in search of my aunt. There were two places she'd most likely be—her room, or in the living area. She'd started to teach the boys domestic duties—cooking from scratch, and basic things such as how to wash dishes or clean a toilet. The boys acted as though they hated it, loud moans of protest always following the cleaning duties, but they seemed to enjoy the cooking. These were things that had been taught prior to my aunt arriving, but she was able to put a feminine flair to their work.

I found her where I thought I would, in the kitchen, elbow deep in flour. She'd have smacked anyone around the head who suggested what she was doing was menial work. Keeping people fed and homes clean was a vital part of society, and anyone who thought it wasn't necessary was an idiot in my aunt's eyes.

"Hey," I said, causing her to glance up from what she was doing. "That looks messy."

Aunt Sarah sighed and didn't respond directly to my comment. "When am I going to get to go home, Darcy? I enjoy helping out here, but I still have a life. I have my business, and my clients are only going to wait for so long."

I reached out and covered the back of her floury hand with mine. "I know, Aunt Sarah. I'll have a word with Devlin and see what he thinks."

Hollan had the memory stick now, which meant his obsession with finding me was now pointless. I had nothing more I could give him, and if he no longer needed to find me, he had nothing to hold over my aunt either. I couldn't see any reason for her not to go home and continue with her life. The house would be hers for as long as she wanted it to be. I knew I wouldn't be going home any time soon. I needed to be here, with the guys. This was my life now, though I knew I'd miss both my aunt and the home I'd grown up in.

"You're leaving again?" she asked, eyeing my jacket.

I nodded. "Yes, I have to go now, but you know I can't say where. I just wanted to say bye."

She exhaled a second sigh through her nose. "I'm going to assume I can't talk you out of it and get you to come home with me, away from all this craziness."

I pursed my lips and shook my head. "I can't. I'm sorry."

"It's those men, isn't it? They've got you under their spell."

My cheeks heated, and I glanced away.

She continued to pound away at the dough. "Can't say I blame you, Darcy." She looked up and caught my eye. "If I was twenty years younger ..." Her cheeks twitched with a held back smile, and she gave me a playful wink.

I laughed, my shoulders relaxing. "Okay, they might be a fringe benefit."

"Just don't go losing your head over some guy," she warned me. "Or guys, for that matter."

"I won't, I promise."

"Any idea how long you'll be gone this time, assuming you don't just hand yourself over to the bad guys again?"

I shrugged. "I'm not totally sure. At least a couple of days, I think. And you be careful down here, too. Nowhere is completely safe right now."

"Which is another reason I think I should go home. I'm not stupid, Darcy. I see people carrying guns when they weren't before. I see how the surveillance has skyrocketed from practically nothing to Fort Knox. It's all to do with Hollan, isn't it?"

I didn't want to give anything away, but I chewed on my lower lip, thinking. She had a point about it being safer back at our house now than it was here.

But Devlin had more important things to think about than my aunt, and I couldn't bother him right now about getting her back home. I wished I'd thought of it earlier. Maybe he could let her take one of the vans so she could drive herself home? I made a mental note to mention it to him before I left.

Time was running out, and I needed to get above ground.

"I really do have to go." I leaned across the counter to place a kiss to my aunt's soft cheek. I slipped my arm around her neck and gave her a quick squeeze. "Love you," I told her. "I'll see you soon."

"See you soon, Darcy, and be careful, okay? Get those men of yours to look after you, and don't do anything reckless."

"I won't, Aunt Sarah."

Why did people keep saying that to me?

Chapter Three

On my way back up to the surface, I stopped where I knew I'd find Devlin.

"What are you doing here, Darcy?" he said as soon as the elevator doors had opened and before I'd even gotten the chance to step out. "The rest of your team is already waiting on top."

A thrill and a sense of pride shot through me from him referring to the guys as the rest of my team. I'd never really belonged to anything before.

"I know. I just wanted to run something by you quickly."

He checked his watch again and frowned. "Better make it fast or they'll leave without you."

That was the last thing I wanted. "I want you to consider letting Sarah take one of the vehicles home. She doesn't belong here, and now Hollan isn't out to get me, she's not in any danger by being out in the real world. If anything, she's probably in more danger by being here, given the situation."

I remembered how Sarah was going to stay with the younger boys should the base come under attack, and experienced a pang of guilt for suggesting she leave them now.

His eyebrows lifted. "I've kind of got more important things to think about than your aunt right now, Darcy, and so do you. I've always told you this isn't a prison, and she's free to leave, if that's what she wants, but considering how things went down last time, I'm not so sure that's a good idea."

I wanted to protect my aunt, but this was bigger than just one person.

I put up both hands. "You're right. I only wanted to throw the idea out there before I left."

He didn't say anything, his eyebrows lifting farther as though daring me to continue.

I backed away, my hands still held in the surrender position. "Okay, okay. I'm going." I didn't want to give him an excuse to tell me to stay, or drop me from the team.

"Bye, Darcy. Stay safe."

"I will." I was back in the elevator car and reached out and hit the button to take me above ground level. I exhaled a long sigh of relief as the doors slid shut, closing off my view of Devlin and the control room. I'd been pushing my luck by stopping to talk to him. I'd always thought Isaac was the dominating, controlling one, but Devlin outranked even Isaac.

The elevator doors slid open again, revealing the greens and browns of the surrounding forest and the almost perfect blue of the sky. It was one of those days where you could feel summer slipping away to fall, a faint nip to the air that wasn't there a week or so ago. Standing around, waiting for me, I guessed, were the guys.

"Come on, Darcy, you'll be late for your own funeral," Clay said, grinning at me as he looked over at me through the curtains of his hair.

I rolled my eyes. "Seriously, don't even joke about that right now."

A number of bags sat at their feet. As well as the bags were several of the silver cases which had displayed the guns and ammo down in the control room. It certainly didn't look as though we'd run short on that front, but I didn't like to think about the situation where we'd need to use them. I'd known how to handle a gun most of my life—my dad being in the FBI had precipitated that—but that didn't mean I liked the things. I was a decent shot, though, and my time in the base had helped. Knowing what I might be going into, I'd made sure I'd spent plenty of time down in the shooting range, and Lorcan had helped me improve my aim. It also meant I got to spend a little one on one time with him, which was a nice fringe benefit.

The plan was that we'd go to the nearest base, warn them, and then we'd have two teams to send to the next two bases, and so on. With each base we warned, we'd gather more men. We'd be able to coordinate our movements, with the final goal being that we'd take down Hollan.

For me, that was the ultimate focus. Yes, I wanted to make sure the other bases were safe, and I was pleased I'd been able to provide them with a way of coordinating with each other, but none of this would be over until Hollan was dead, and I wouldn't rest until I made that happen.

"It's a shame the memory stick didn't contain the phone numbers of the other bases, rather than the locations," Clay quipped. "It would have made warning everyone about Hollan a hell of a lot easier."

"It would also mean Hollan wouldn't know where to find the other bases," I pointed out.

Isaac frowned. "He'd have been able to use the phone numbers anyway. He'd have the equipment to track them. But there was never any point in putting phone numbers on there. Phone numbers change."

"Locations of things change, too," Alex pointed out. "We don't know for sure that the bases are still in the same places they were six years ago. When everyone went dark, some of them might have gotten spooked and moved locations."

Isaac shook his head. "Unlikely. Unless they had a reason for doing so that we're unaware of, no one would move a setup like this voluntarily. Think of all the technology and infrastructure. Plus, if they moved, they would have destroyed the one chance of getting in touch with the other bases again."

I sighed and put my hands on my hips. "Okay, so we just go and hope we can find the locations before Hollan does."

I hated that I'd let that son of a bitch get away. I turned every moment of what had happened over in my head, trying to figure out if there was something I could have done differently. I should have grabbed the gun and shot him. I should have run faster.

"This isn't all down to you, Darcy," Kingsley reminded me. "We were all there, too. You weren't the only one who wanted to stop him."

He was right, of course. I didn't know why I constantly felt as though it was me against Hollan.

"I guess it's because I know he killed my father," I admitted. "We have a history. That bastard used to come to my house, bring us gifts, and drink beer with my dad. And the whole time he was living this other life that went completely against what my dad believed in. I know this is bigger than just me and him, but it feels personal."

He placed his hand on my shoulder. "I get it, Darcy, but you have to remember you're part of a team now. Our team. We have to work together."

I nodded. "Yeah, and we will. We're good together, I know that, but that doesn't stop me from wanting to get my hands on Hollan."

"And we will," he assured me.

I looked around for one of the vans, and then back down at all the bags. "Are we going to have to carry all these down to the transport?"

Isaac frowned at me. "That's not the kind of transport we're getting."

"It's not? What are—" A familiar sound cut off my words. I frowned back at Isaac, my brain trying to piece together why I recognized it, and then realization dawned, and with it came an unnerving stomach flip.

"Oh, shit. We're traveling by helicopter?"

"Yep." He looked a little smug, pushing his hands into his pants pockets.

"I've never been in a helicopter," I admitted. "And I'm kind of not great with heights."

Kingsley laughed and stooped to pick up two big bags, one in each hand. "Don't worry, we'll protect you."

I was doubtful. "Protect me from falling hundreds of feet to my death? How are you going to do that? Act like my cushion when I hit the ground?"

He flashed me white teeth and a wink. "Anything for you."

Clay pushed his hand through his hair. "You're not going to fall, sugar. These things have doors, you know."

"And anyway," Lorcan agreed, shrugging his shoulders in his leather jacket. "Even if they didn't, gravity still works in the up and down direction, not sideways. As long as the chopper doesn't roll, you're not going anywhere."

"It's the rolling I'm worried about."

Clay jabbed me in the side playfully. "You can hold on to me if we roll."

My eyes widened. "Is that likely to happen?"

Isaac stepped in. "No, it's not, and like Clay says, this one has doors."

The sound of the chopper grew louder, the thwacking of blades through the air. Then it appeared at the point where the trees met the horizon, and I instinctively ducked. The chopper was massive, far bigger than the one I'd seen before.

"This one is designed to take sixteen people," Isaac yelled over the noise of the helicopter. "So it can easily take us and all the equipment."

"How long will it take us to get to the first location?" I shouted back.

"It flies at around one hundred and sixty miles per hour, so maybe two or three hours, depending on the headwind."

Two or three hours on that thing? I barely wanted to contemplate it. But it did mean we'd be reaching the first location within a few hours rather than half a day, which was how long it would have taken us by road. I knew Hollan had access to helicopters, too. If this was a race to get there first, we'd just evened the stakes a little.

We all stepped back as the huge machine hovered above us. The area was clear of trees, but there were still multiple items of rusting machinery dotted around from when this used to be an old logging facility. I knew the pilot of the chopper wouldn't risk getting its blades caught in anything. At least there weren't any overhead lines around here. The electricity and phone lines to the base had been run underground to prevent anyone wondering why so much access to technology would be needed all the way out here.

The wind caused by the blades sent my hair whipping from my face, and the front of my clothes appeared glued to my body. I didn't miss the way Clay's gaze slipped down every curve on view, and then gave me a smirk. The hit on the head didn't seem to have affected his sex drive any. Not that I minded.

Leaves and twigs from the forest floor were lifted into the air and flung at us as the chopper descended. I raised my arm to shield my face and turned away slightly, trying to protect myself from the dirt and small stones pinging against any exposed skin, thankful for the jeans, boots, and jacket I wore. I noted the guys were all doing the same. Despite my fears about riding in the helicopter, I didn't want to look like the weaker species in front of the others.

The helicopter landing skids finally made contact with the ground, and, as they did, the spinning of the blades began to slow. I was able to look around again.

The door opened, and the pilot jumped out. "You my team?" he called out over the still noisy helicopter.

Isaac nodded and stepped forward to shake his hand. "I'm Isaac."

"Jonathan," the pilot introduced himself.

Isaac pointed to each of the guys, and named them in turn. Then he ended with me. "And this is Darcy."

I stepped forward to shake the pilot's hand. I guessed we'd be spending a fair amount of time together if this was how we were going to get around to each of the bases.

"Good to meet you, Darcy." He was in his late twenties, I guessed. Blue eyes and military short hair. I wondered what he thought of me with all these men.

With introductions done, we set about hauling the bags of weapons and equipment into the back of the helicopter. I helped, not wanting anyone to think I wasn't capable of pulling my weight. I was relieved to see the aircraft did have doors, and, as we climbed in, one by one, my relief grew to see harness style seatbelts attached to each of the seats as well. They wouldn't do us much good if the helicopter fell out of the sky in a ball of flames, but at least the falling out part could be put out of my mind. My legs still felt weak and shaky as I climbed on board and took a seat between Clay and Lorcan. The smell of diesel and heated metal filled my nostrils. There were three rows of seats, and Isaac took up position directly behind the pilot. Kingsley and Alex climbed into the row behind us. Each seat also had a set of noise canceling headphones behind it, and, once I'd strapped myself into the seat with the harness, I reached out and pulled the headphones over my ears.

Immediately, the noisy roar from the chopper was dulled. We had small mouthpieces attached where we could talk to each other.

Once everyone was inside, Jonathan shut the door, encasing us inside the helicopter's body. He moved to the front of the aircraft and climbed back into the pilot's seat. He pulled on his own headphones, and I jumped as his voice suddenly blared in my ears.

"Everyone strapped in and ready to go?"

We all nodded obediently.

Because the helicopter had only been idling while we'd climbed on board, it took seconds for the pilot to get the huge beast moving again. My stomach lurched as it lifted off the ground, then it tilted, and a small scream escaped my throat. I reached out and grabbed the hands of the two men on either side of me, anchoring myself down with them. I needed to pull myself together. How was I going to face things far worse if I was allowing a helicopter ride to freak me out? I didn't want to look out of the window at the massive distance that continued to grow between us and the ground. I knew we were going to be up high, but it didn't feel natural to be inside a little tin can in the middle of the air.

On either side of me, Clay and Lorcan exchanged a smirk. I jabbed the pair of them with an elbow each in the side, and then spoke into the mouthpiece attached to the headphones.

"Look, this is my first time, okay? I'm allowed to be a little nervous."

Clay grinned. "I'm just glad to see the fearless one has something that unnerves her."

"I'm not fearless!" I protested. There were times when I felt as though everything frightened me.

"No? Says the woman who hands herself over to an armed man who wants her dead, or thinks nothing about stabbing someone if they get in her way."

"That was different," I pointed out. "They were asking for it."

My thoughts went to Otto. I wondered what had happened to him after we'd left him at the hospital. I prayed he'd survived his wounds. He'd seemed like a tough guy, and I felt sure he would have. Had he gone home to Sweden, or was he still somewhere in the country? Was he still on Hollan's payroll, or had he cut himself off from that contract? I thought it would be pretty awkward for him to continue to work with Hollan considering he'd helped me escape.

The helicopter climbed higher into the sky, the force pushing me back into my seat, and then finally leveled off. I breathed a sigh of relief. I didn't know why, but I felt better now we were heading forward rather than up.

I tried to relax. I had a good couple of hours ahead of me, and I'd be an anxious mess by the time we reached the first location. I tried not to think too hard about what might be waiting for us when we got there.

Chapter Four

O nce my initial fear had abated, it was replaced with a kind of anxious boredom. There was nothing else to do except look out the window and watch the country go by far below. The threads of highways with tiny dots of cars. The squared clusters of buildings, and the sporadic blue oblongs of backyard pools. Occasionally, the windows of the chopper turned white as we passed through a cloud, but then the clear sky would be back again. Due to cloud cover, we hadn't been able to get a decent satellite view of the area we were heading to. I hoped we didn't get a turn in the weather the farther we traveled. I didn't like the idea of being up here during a storm, and I figured any sign of lightning would ground us.

Isaac's voice sounded in my ear. "Only thirty minutes to go."

I knew the others had heard, too. We exchanged glances, and from the sudden change in atmosphere, I got the impression they were also anxious about what we'd find. We would need to convince whoever was in charge of this place that the threat we perceived was both imminent and very real. We also needed their manpower to help warn the other bases. We'd cover more ground if there were more of us.

"When are we going to know we're there?" I asked through the headset.

The pilot replied. "The helicopter's GPS is pretty sophisticated. I just plugged in the coordinates you needed, and it takes us right there." At the mention of the coordinates, the numbers flashed up in the airspace around me, some of them even appearing on the other side of the window of the helicopter, so they literally floated in midair. It was a strangely disorienting experience.

Beneath us, the patchwork of different shades of green—olives, limes, and emeralds—gave way to the expanse of a dark blue lake.

"We're almost there." Isaac twisted around to face us. "The cloud cover finally seems to have cleared from that area. Lorcan, you've got the thermal imaging equipment. I'm not sure we're going to need it, but just in case."

Lorcan leaned down to the bag at his feet and started to pull out the equipment.

I craned my neck to look out the window, down to the ground below. There didn't seem to be anything around, but I reminded myself that our base would appear much the same way if someone was to view it from above. The whole point was that these places were secret and hard to find. It wasn't as though they'd have a neon sign with an arrow pointing it out.

A white oblong stood out starkly against the dark green of the vegetation and the deep blue of the lake.

"What's that?" I shouted, pointing down.

"I think that's where we're heading," Clay called back.

It was right on the bank where the lake met the shore. As we got closer, I spotted a large dam built across the lake, and several electrical towers rose into the air. What I was looking at dawned on me. It was a hydropower station.

"Do you think that's it? Does it line up with the coordinates?"

"Yeah, sure does," the pilot called back. "You want me to put her down?"

It took me a moment to realize the 'her' he was talking about was the chopper.

"Let's just fly over," Isaac said. "Get an idea if there's anything else we should be aware of."

The pilot nodded. "There's a lot of tree coverage, too. This baby's got a rotor diameter of over fifty feet. I need to find a decent place to land."

Isaac looked back to us. "And I want everyone armed and ready to go, just in case."

We all immediately bent to the bags and cases containing the weapons. I'd upgraded myself to a sub-automatic Berretta—a handgun of a decent size for me to handle, but one that packed a bit more punch than I'd been using previously. The gun felt good to hold, a little insurance against what might happen next. We weren't expecting the inhabitants of this base to give us any trouble, but it was always best to be prepared. I added a couple of magazines into my jacket pockets. I hoped I wouldn't need to fire a single shot, never mind need to reload, but like Isaac said, it was for just in case.

Though there were no obvious signs of life down at the power station, Lorcan was already working the thermal surveillance equipment. It looked like a combination between a camera and a set of binoculars, but I knew it would be able to tell Lorcan if there was any sign of human habitation down there. He pressed the goggles to his eyes and peered at the area below us.

The pilot banked the chopper to the right, and I was thankful for both the doors and the harness belt as we leaned. We continued to fly, circling the perimeter of the building. I forced myself to look, despite my stomach lurching at the height. A single road led in and out of the power station, but I couldn't see any signs of people or vehicles on the move.

"It may not look like there's any life down there," Lorcan said, removing the goggles from his eyes, "but the place is glowing up like an atomic bomb. Even if those aren't heat signatures from people, there's energy coming from somewhere."

I reached out and took the equipment from him. Leaning over Lorcan's lap so I could see out of the window, no longer caring about the height, I placed the goggles to my eyes. He was right. The whole of the building, which previously appeared like a white rectangle against all the blue and green, now glowed orange. I scanned the surrounding area, trying to pick up on any smaller dots of color, wondering if there might be people taking shelter among all the foliage, or perhaps even a couple of vehicles on the road which we weren't able to spot from up here, but there was nothing.

I removed the goggles and handed them back to Lorcan. "Looks quiet, though."

He nodded in agreement. "Hmm. Almost too quiet."

"Our base would look quiet, too, if someone were to observe it from above," Kingsley said from behind me, leaning forward against the back of my seat so his forearms brushed my shoulder.

"True," I agreed.

"I can set her down on the dam," Jonathan called out to us. "It looks pretty sturdy from here."

It wasn't some rickety wooden contraption. The dam appeared to be solid concrete. Because of its proximity to the water, there was no tree coverage to worry about, so it would make it safer for the helicopter to land.

Assuming we even had the right place, if this base was anything like ours, they'd have cameras and would see us coming. The noise of the chopper also gave us away. One advantage helicopters didn't have was that they weren't exactly stealth-like, and this was a big machine. They would have heard us coming from miles away.

The pilot began to descend, and the closer we got to landing, the greater my nerves increased. I didn't like how quiet it was, despite telling myself it was what we'd expected. I kept reminding myself these were our allies, and we were there to help them, and warn them. They would be pleased to see us, and learn the locations of each of the training bases had been revealed again. Previously, the locations were kept as a top secret before they were leaked, but I figured that must be all out the window now. They needed to be able to coordinate with each other to take out the threat of Hollan and his men. What would happen afterward, however, I didn't know. I assumed they'd make more of a backup plan, though, to prevent such a thing happening again.

The downward thrust of air from the chopper caused the water from the lake to spray out and up the closer we got, until it felt as though we were surrounded by a cloud of fine, white mist. I briefly wondered what would happen if the dam didn't hold. Did these things land on water and float? I hoped I wasn't going to find out.

Jonathan had landed so the side of the chopper faced the shore. This meant we were able to open the door on Lorcan's side and climb out without trying to navigate the helicopter. Above us, the rotor began to slow.

"You wait here," Isaac told the pilot. "Be ready to leave."

Jonathan nodded. "I'll keep her warmed up."

We climbed out, each of us armed. Everyone was on high alert, but, despite the unsubtle arrival, no one had come out to greet us. Were people watching us from inside, wondering what we were doing, and trying to assess if we were a threat? We didn't exactly look like a group of friends out on a pleasure ride. With the guys, there was no hiding the fact they were trained for combat.

Isaac led the way. As well as the weapon held in one hand, he had the bag containing his laptop strapped across his chest. Kingsley and Lorcan moved in front of me, Clay and Alex coming up from behind. I felt like I was the filling in a man sandwich, but I wasn't going to complain.

"Stay in the middle, Darcy," Isaac called out. "We've got you protected from every angle."

Okay, maybe I did want to complain. That I was a member of the team now, and they didn't need to protect me was what I wanted to complain about, but now wasn't the time. We needed to keep our wits about us, not start arguing, and I knew they would give me an argument.

The building looked a hell of a lot bigger from the ground than it had from above. I couldn't hear the sound of any engines powering the station. In fact, other than the noise of the chopper, the place was eerily quiet. But, from the thermal imaging, we knew it was being used, so something was going on here. Just like at our base, there were numerous signs around warning people to stay out.

Lorcan rubbed his hand over his mouth as we crept forward. "Looks to me like someone built this place, but never got it up and running."

"Maybe they were worried the water was going to dry up," Clay threw in. Lorcan raised his eyebrows at him, and Clay shrugged. "Or maybe not."

"You think it might have been built as a disguise for the base?" I suggested.

Isaac nodded. "Looks that way to me."

Kingsley joined in with a nod, but his was slow and thoughtful. When he spoke, it was with admiration. "We used something that was no longer in use, and they used something that hadn't started to be used yet. I like it."

I wondered what the other places would be disguised as when we found them.

Ignoring the keep out signs, we moved deeper into the area surrounding the building for the hydropower plant. I was still surprised no one had come to ask us who we were and what we were doing yet, but maybe they were laying low until they could figure out what we wanted, and if we were friend or foe.

"The entrance is over here." Isaac jerked his chin in the direction of large double doors set into the front of the building.

He got closer, us following behind, but staying alert.

Then he drew to a halt, his hand held aloft to tell us to wait.

I craned forward to see what had made him stop. The entrance was ajar.

Clay pulled a face. "Did anyone put out the welcome mat?"

"Move with caution," Isaac said, ignoring his comment.

I kind of figured that was what we were doing, but wasn't going to say so. We crept closer to the walls, rather than stand in front of the ajar doorway, protecting ourselves from anyone who might start shooting from inside the building. We all had our weapons drawn.

Isaac lifted a finger again. We were all pressed up against the wall, then he stepped forward, weapon raised as he stepped into the open doorway. I heard his reaction before I saw the cause of it.

"Ah, shit."

No shots were fired, so I followed him in. Lorcan and Clay moved with me, flanking my shoulders. Kingsley and Alex brought up the rear. We were all inside when I saw what had caused Isaac's reaction. My stomach turned. On the floor lay a man sprawled facedown. A smear of blood stood out starkly against the white of the stone floor.

The words escaped my mouth, even though I was pointing out the obvious. "He's been shot."

Isaac looked over his shoulder toward me, his eyebrows pulled down in a frown of concern. "Yes, but who by?"

Kingsley's expression matched Isaac's. "That's what we need to worry about."

A new level of tension infected the group. I felt it radiating from each of the men. My body vibrated with nerves, and my stomach churned. My mouth ran so dry my tongue felt fat, but I forced myself to lick my lips and swallow hard, trying to push down my anxiety. Together, we left the body and moved in deeper.

Only a little farther on, we found two more men, also dead, in much the same position as the first. An unnerving certainty was creeping through me.

"You think they turned on each other?" I asked, keeping my voice low and still hoping the worst thing possible might not have happened.

Clay lifted his eyebrows at me. "That's pretty damned unlikely, don't you think?"

"So what do you think happened?" I stared at him, willing him to say something that didn't include the man I hated most.

Clay didn't grant my wishes. "That Hollan got here before us."

Chapter Five

C lay's words sank into our small group, and Isaac's lips thinned. "I'd hoped we weren't going to have to consider that."

Shit.

Alex stepped in. "You think they might still be here?"

Isaac's gaze shifted to the tall, blond doctor. "I want to say no, but we need to stay vigilant. They might have heard the chopper landing and decided to lay low until they'd figured out how many we were and what resources we had."

Alex nodded. "Agreed."

The entrance hall divided off in two directions, left and right. In front of us was a door. A small glass window in the door revealed the stairwell beyond.

"We should split up." Kingsley jerked his chin toward the door. "We'll cover more ground that way. I'll take the stairs with Darcy. Isaac and Alex, head left. Clay and Lorcan, you guys go right. We'll reconvene here. Any sign of trouble, fire a shot into the air, and the rest of us will come running."

I was touched that Kingsley chose for me to be the one he partnered with, but then it occurred to me that maybe it was simply that he was the biggest, and I was the smallest, so he was evening things out a little. But I preferred to think he wanted to protect me. I had to admit, as I pressed close to him as we pushed through the doors and into the stairwell, I did feel comforted having his big presence beside me. Lorcan was the weapons guy, and probably knew how to shoot better than anyone, but there was something primal about having Kingsley's bulk sheltering me.

He paused in the stairwell. "Up or down?"

My lips twisted. "Down."

He nodded, and we got moving again. I covered him from behind as we made our way down the stairs, into the basement of the building. Halfway down, a fourth body lay slumped across the stairs, as though he'd been running and was shot from behind, sending him flying down the remaining steps. The thought caused a shudder to wrack through me, and I whipped my head back around, making sure the staircase was still empty.

So far, other than the dead men, I hadn't seen anything that made me think this was a base like the one we'd left.

"Could we be in the wrong place?" I hissed to Kingsley. If we were, maybe Hollan had found the wrong place too, and killed everyone, assuming it was one of the bases. I didn't know how to feel about that. I'd be happy if the base remained undiscovered by Hollan, but I didn't like the thought that innocent people had died.

Kingsley nudged something with his foot. "Only if energy workers go around armed," he replied.

I looked down. The thing he'd nudged was a gun. "Let's keep going."

A second set of doors met us at the bottom of the staircase. Kingsley positioned himself on one side of them and nodded for me to stand on the other. I held my gun, ready to start shooting if needed.

Kingsley stepped out and kicked open the doors. They revealed a second corridor beyond, but the space was empty. He stepped through, and I followed. On the wall, a security lock had been disarmed.

We continued. Numerous doors led off the hallway. The first door we tried led onto a room filled with computers and monitors, all destroyed, pieces of glass and plastic all over the floor. Chairs had been toppled, and screens smashed. There were another couple of bodies, too, slumped at their desks, bullet holes in the backs of their heads.

Nausea swelled up inside me. This was exactly what I'd been frightened of. That Hollan would come here, and they wouldn't be prepared in the slightest. Hollan's men had taken them by surprise and killed them all.

"Where are the boys?" I asked Kingsley, my voice coming out choked. This place was a training site, just like our base, and there would be the chosen boys here that they were training.

Kingsley wouldn't meet my eye and shook his head, his nostrils flaring, his full lips pressing together. "I don't know."

I knew what he was thinking—that they were dead, too.

I covered my face with the hand not holding the gun. "Oh, God."

"Go back upstairs," he told me. "Find the others and tell them what we've found. It looks like Hollan's men have done what they intended and are long gone."

But I shook my head. "No, I'm staying."

I knew Kingsley was trying to protect me from what we might find, but I didn't deserve protecting. I'd been partially responsible for Hollan getting away with the memory stick. I was responsible for what had happened here. I wasn't going to turn away from it now. Still, the thought of coming across the bodies of the boys made my stomach crawl into my throat. I pictured all the boys back at the base, and imagined finding them in the same way, and tears pricked the backs of my eyes. This was what we were fighting.

My legs felt weak, but I pushed on, following Kingsley's back as we moved from room to room. We discovered a setup much like the one we had, only on one level rather than several. We walked down the corridor, checking each doorway. Every muscle in my body was so tense, the ache spread through my neck and shoulders. My fingers wanted to tremble around the grip of my gun, but I held on tight to stop them.

Through a set of swinging double doors, we found an industrial kitchen with a dining hall leading off of it. But there were no bodies of children, and nothing that gave us any clue as to what had happened here, so we moved on.

Another door led to the sleeping quarters. Unlike our base, where we had our own rooms, this layout was done in the form of dormitories. Bunk beds were positioned against each wall, the rooms providing accommodation for at least six people. I wondered how many lived down here. I had assumed it would be the same size as our base, but, now I was here, I could see it was smaller. These rooms had clearly been lived in. Clothes were piled on top of one of the beds. A book sat beside another. CDs had been stacked on the floor. My initial hopes that maybe they were no longer training in this base vanished. I didn't know where the bodies of the boys were, but this setup definitely made it look as though they'd been down here.

We shook our heads and shrugged at each other, both equally baffled.

"Where are they?" I asked Kingsley.

His brow furrowed. "Could they all be adults now? Maybe this base hadn't taken on any new recruits for a while."

"There must be a way to find out. Paperwork, perhaps?"

"Yeah, maybe. Perhaps the others have found something."

A sudden metal clang made us both stand to attention. We exchanged a glance. What was that? The other guys making their way down here? But it didn't sound like feet. It sounded like something metal had been knocked over in the kitchen.

We broke into a run, heading back toward the noise.

Kingsley glanced back at me. "It came from the kitchen."

Double swinging doors led onto the kitchen—a large space of mainly white tiles and stainless steel. A steel island was in the center of the room, creating extra work space and offering storage with cupboards, also in stainless steel, below. We paused outside the doors, ready with our guns, Kingsley leading the way. He counted us in silently, lifting his fingers... *one, two, three.*

At three, we burst through the double doors, weapons aimed. My gaze searched the space, trying to see where the sound had come from. Things didn't fall over by themselves.

A muffled sob filtered to my ears.

Kingsley and I exchanged a confused glance.

Instinct told me that whoever had made the sound wasn't someone we were going to need to use guns against.

I lowered my weapon.

"Hello?" I called softly. "Is someone there?"

No one answered, but from somewhere behind the central island, there came a sniff. We'd checked behind there when we'd done our first round.

I frowned, stepping forward. Kingsley did the same, taking the opposite direction, so we covered the island from both sides. We both stepped out into the gap between the island and the rear counters, but the space was clear. I frowned up at Kingsley, but then I heard it again, the faintest hitch of breath. I placed my fingers to my lips then pointed at one of the closed cupboard doors. The cupboards were the same height as the counter, and easily big enough to hide a child.

"We know you're in there," I said, keeping my voice gentle. "It's okay. We're friends. You can come out now. We're not going to hurt you."

I didn't know how much the person hiding inside the stainless steel cupboard had seen, but it was enough to make him continue to hide, despite us saying we were friends. I guessed he had no way of knowing. Maybe Hollan had said the same thing when he was trying to coax them all into the open. I gritted my teeth as a sudden surge of anger rose inside of me. That son of a bitch.

With no other choice, I reached out and took the handle and pulled it open.

A small bundle charged at me with a roar of fury and something held in his hand. Thank God, I managed to restrain my instinct to shoot, and instead lifted the gun up to block the blow. But something else happened in the madness. The whirling dervish trying to attack me was suddenly pulled backward. I was able to put my senses back together again.

The person who'd come flying out of the cupboard looked to be a boy of about seven years old. The thing he held in his hands was a rolling pin. Kingsley now held him around the waist, and he reached out and plucked the rolling pin from the boy's hands and threw it to the side. The pin hit the floor with a loud clatter and rolled a couple of times before coming to a halt. The boy wiggled and squirmed, but he was no match for Kingsley.

"Hey, quit it, kid. We're your friends, I swear."

I nodded, trying to catch the boy's eye. "We've come from a place like this one. What's your name?"

"George," the boy muttered, continuing to throw his shoulders back and forth to dislodge Kingsley.

"What happened here, George?" he asked.

George seemed to realize we weren't trying to hurt him and shook his head. "I don't know. The alarms went off, and then there was lots of shouting and gunshots. I know I should have helped, but then I saw Mitchell on the floor, and he was dead—"

The boy's voice broke, and he slumped in Kingsley's arms. Tears streamed down his cheeks, and Kingsley relaxed his grip, lowering to a crouch to bring himself more level with the child.

"Who's Mitchell?" he asked. "One of the other boys?"

George shook his head then sniffed and wiped his sleeve across his nose, leaving a thin trail of silver across the blue material. "No, he was one of our trainers."

"Where are all the other boys?" I asked. "The ones you were training with? Are they hiding, too?"

He shook his head. "No, they're gone."

"Gone where?"

He looked up at us, his blue eyes wide and appearing too large in his small face. "The people who came here—the ones with the guns—they took them."

Chapter Six

The heavy footfall of multiple men running down the corridor toward us drew our eyes toward the entrance. My heart jackknifed in my chest. Kingsley stood again and aimed his gun toward the double doors, and George cowered behind him.

The door pushed open, revealing the other guys. Isaac, Alex, Lorcan, and Clay.

"Hey, there you are," said Clay, taking a couple of swaggered steps toward us. Then he spotted George and stopped. "Who's this?"

"George," I said. "He's the only one left of the boys."

Horror passed across each of the men's faces, and I realized what I'd said. "No, they're not dead." At least, I hoped they weren't. "George says Hollan's men took them."

Isaac frowned. "Took them? Why would he do that?"

I shook my head. "I don't know." My mind whirled. Why the hell would Hollan take the boys? What was he planning on doing with them? I assumed it would be nothing good.

"How many other boys were down here with you?" Isaac asked George.

"There's five of us. Me, Tad—who is only six—and Xander, who is eleven. Then there's Scott, who's the same age as Xander, and Chris, who is twelve."

I felt the guys glance between them. I knew what they were thinking. The five boys were just like they'd been years ago when they'd been doing their training. It must be hard for them not to put themselves in the boys' places. My heart ached at the thought of those four boys being dragged out of here by armed men, most likely being forced to step over the bodies of the men who'd trained and raised them for the majority of their lives. They would be terrified, and despite what training they may have been given so far, it would mean nothing against Hollan's men.

Where were they now? Where would Hollan have taken them? Back to D.C.? I found it hard to imagine. Was this his way of punishing us somehow? Was he going to use the boys against us?

Again, the uncomfortable gnawing feeling gnashed its teeth in my gut. I'd said to Devlin that I felt things had gotten too personal between me and Hollan, and that even though he wanted to destroy the training bases, he would want to get his own back on me as well. I prayed this wasn't going to be his way of doing it.

"How do we know where Hollan is going next?" Lorcan's face was rigid with anger, his jaw locked. I knew this side of him now, the angry side, the side that made him dangerous, where he wanted to kill and break things. "Hell, he could already be there. He might be slaughtering another base right now while we're standing around here talking."

"Right," Isaac said, taking charge. "We need to be methodical. This place has cameras, and yes, they would have been disarmed, but not initially. They might give us some idea of how many men Hollan brought with him, or even what kind of transport they're using. If they're traveling by car, that buys us more time. We need to get back to the control room and see what we can pull up."

"A lot of it was smashed," I said.

"Hopefully it was only the monitors. If the hard drives are intact, I'll be able to attach my laptop, and we can view the surveillance on there."

It sounded like a plan, and at least it felt as though we might have something more to go on than just a stab in the dark.

"Keep your eyes peeled for anything that doesn't look like it belongs here either," Isaac continued. "Darcy, you come with me in case there's anything that needs to be memorized. Alex and Lorcan, you go to each of the bodies and check them over. There's a chance one or two of them might be Hollan's men and were taken down first. Check their pockets for ID, or anything else that might help us. Clay, you go back to the chopper and tell them we'll be leaving within the next fifteen minutes, and to be ready. We've probably already wasted too much time. Kingsley, you stay with the boy."

Kingsley's eyebrows lifted at the prospect of being put on babysitting duty, but he didn't complain. Besides, the kid seemed to have taken a liking to him, and was sticking to the big man's side. It didn't look as though George would have gone with anyone else, even if Isaac had ordered it.

Together, we left the kitchen, and then separated again, Lorcan and Alex going to check the bodies over, while Clay went back to the helicopter.

"George," Isaac said to the boy, "I know this is hard for you, but it's really important that you tell us if you heard or saw anything that might give us a clue where those men took your friends. Can you think back, and try to remember if you saw anything important? You can look at the video on my computer soon, too, if I can upload the surveillance footage, and tell me if you know or recognize anything or anyone."

The boy pressed his knuckles to his lips and nodded. "They said something about it being five miles away?"

"Who did?"

"The men who took the others. They said something about it being five miles—" He stopped himself and shook his head. "No, not five miles. Five *hundred* miles."

Isaac and I exchanged a glance.

"We need to find out what transport they were in. We might be able to predict where they were going next if we can."

I bit my lower lip. If they were traveling by helicopter, too, and they were already ahead of us, we'd never catch up.

"Can't Devlin send someone else in to intercept them?" I asked. "Surely there must be people who are closer who can help."

Isaac shook his head. "This is the exact reason we needed to be back in touch with each of the bases. There is no one else. Only us. To everyone else, Hollan looks like the authority. He's the good guy. It's not as though we can call the cops on him."

I motioned around us. "But what about all of this? Surely the police will listen when they see the bodies."

"And how are we going to explain it? For one, our cover will be blown. What we do will no longer be a secret, and if it's not a secret, there's no point in us even existing. Plus, if we contact the cops now and they show up here, all that's going to happen is that we'll get pulled in for questioning, and Hollan will be free to complete his plan."

Isaac was right. I ground my teeth in frustration, wishing there was something more we could do.

He marched back to the tech room, and I followed, forced to break into a jog to keep up with him. It was exactly how we'd left it, with screens smashed, desks and chairs toppled over. Hollan's men didn't only want to kill the people who worked here, or take the boys they were training. No, they were sending a message. This was their way of letting us know they were winning, and that they wouldn't leave any part of the bases standing. My thought went to our base, and to Aunt Sarah, and the boys she was helping to take care of. Was this to be their fate, too? The idea of returning only to discover a similar scene caused ice to slip through my veins, chilling me to the core.

Isaac stood with his hands on his hips, surveying the remains of the technology the room housed. He knew far more about computers than I ever would, probably recognizing things that meant nothing to me, then he stepped forward and got to work, flicking switches and checking leads. He flipped one switch and something came to life, light appearing behind the buttons.

"Gotcha," he said, mainly to himself.

He started moving things around, connecting and disconnecting different leads. He certainly looked like he knew what he was doing, but I was clueless.

Finally, he pulled his laptop out from the bag strapped across his chest and used some of the leads he'd found to attach the laptop to what looked to be one of the system units of the bigger machines. He righted one of the chairs—a small leather one with wheels on the bottom—and sat down.

"Let's hope this is the right one," he said, though again I was sure he was talking to himself.

He fired up his laptop and started to scroll through the files. He clicked on one. "Bingo."

The stairwell came up in grainy color. Isaac scrolled, forwarding through the times. There was a flash of movement as someone walked up the stairs, but it wasn't anything interesting. How long ago had they been here? How much time had we missed them by? How long had George been hiding in the kitchen cupboard? It occurred to me that if we'd left an hour earlier, we might well have walked right into this. We might have been able to help, or alternatively, they would have heard the chopper coming and been ready to take us down the minute our feet touched the ground.

Sudden movement flashed on screen, and a man flew backward, landing on the stairs in the position we'd found him. Then more men ran past, leaping over the body. How many were there? Was Hollan among them?

Isaac jabbed his finger at the time stamp. "They were here almost two hours ago. That helps us narrow things down."

"Good." It was a relief that he seemed to know what he was doing.

Isaac opened more files, bringing up more video footage of other parts of the base. He appeared to be looking for something in particular, but his face was a mask of concentration, and I couldn't predict what.

Then footage of the outside of the building and the surrounding area appeared on screen.

I watched in stunned horror as multiple black vans screeched to the front of the building. The doors opened and men dressed in Kevlar body armor and helmets jumped out. Each man was armed and moving with fast, silent precision. They looked as though they were taking on a terrorist cell.

Though horrified at what I was seeing, there was one bright light.

"They're traveling by road," I said, noting the presence of the vans.

Isaac nodded. "It's a small bonus, but it's one we should be able to take advantage of."

"Can we tell which one is Hollan? Is he with them?"

I studied each of the figures on screen, hoping there would be something that would distinguish him from the others. But they each wore the same black protective vests and helmets. Identical soldiers.

"This might not be his only team," Isaac said. "He might have sent multiple teams out at the same time. He might not even have been here. There's a chance he's gone to a different location."

"That's possible. But how many people does he have access to? Yes, he's an FBI agent, and he almost certainly has a number of men behind him who are as corrupt as he is, but multiple teams of men?"

Isaac frowned. "He could have lied to them. We know that wouldn't exactly be against his moral code. I might have told them they were dealing with something corrupt—assuming these men are aboveboard."

My teeth dug into my lower lip. "I guess that's the real question. Do these men know what they're really doing—the truth of who they're killing—or have they been fed a pack of lies? If it's lies, and they don't realize what they're doing, they might be easier to stop."

Isaac nodded. "But if they know the full truth of the situation, it'll be kill or be killed."

I didn't like the sound of that.

The door pushed open, and Alex and Lorcan entered the room. Isaac twisted in his seat. "Did you find anything on the bodies?"

Lorcan shook his head. "Not a single thing. It was as though someone deliberately went over them and made sure there wasn't anything identifying them. I'm surprised they didn't take the tips of their fingers and their teeth as well."

"It wouldn't make any difference if they did. These men work off grid, just like we do. We wouldn't find any records to identify them by."

Alex frowned and folded his arms across his chest. "If any of them were Hollan's men, they'll probably have a record somewhere."

I thought of Otto and how Hollan had recruited him to do a job. There was a chance Hollan had done the same thing with these men, and they were guns for hire.

Isaac uploaded the video files to his laptop, then unplugged from the system unit.

He got to his feet. "We can't do much more here. We need to get on the move and see if we can catch up with the son of a bitch."

"And get the boys back," I said, hoping we weren't too late. What the hell did he want with a bunch of kids, anyway? Yes, they were being trained, but they wouldn't be the final product until they were grown men like Isaac and the others.

Even so, I was glad to be leaving this place. I followed Isaac, Lorcan, and Alex out of the destroyed control room and back into the stairwell. I averted my gaze from the body still slumped on the stairs as we retraced our route up the stairs and into the big entrance hall where the other three bodies lay. It felt wrong to leave them, but what else could we do? I stepped into fresh air and allowed myself to breathe again.

Kingsley had been waiting outside with George. The boy stood at Kingsley's side, glancing around nervously. I wondered how often he'd been allowed up. Had the boys been allowed to explore the area, to run in the surrounding forests and swim in the lake, like those back at the home base were? He looked nervous, like a beaten dog just released from its chains, but I didn't know if that was because he was worried because of the attack, or if it was the sudden exposure to wide open space that was bothering him.

Then he caught sight of the helicopter and his eyes widened. "Are we going for a ride in that?"

"Sure are," said Kingsley. "You ever been in one before?"

He shook his head. "No, sir."

"It's pretty cool."

"Sure is!"

The boy's nerves seemed to have been forgotten at the prospect of a ride in the helicopter.

I took Isaac to one side. "What's the plan? Are we going after Hollan, or are we going to the next base?"

"I think the two things are the same. According to the coordinates, and George overhearing them saying it was five hundred miles away, that'll take us to the next base, which makes me think that's where they're going, too. We could try to catch up with Hollan on the road, but, if somehow we fail, they'll be free to continue and repeat what they've done here."

"So you think we should head for the second base, and hope we get there before Hollan does?"

He nodded. "At least that way they'll be prepared should Hollan and his men arrive."

"We just have to get there first."

"That's the challenge. They have a couple of hours on us, but we can move twice as fast."

I sucked in a breath and nodded. I prayed we'd be on time. The idea of coming across a similar scene at the next base tore me up inside. I didn't know the people there, but that didn't stop me from caring about them. I didn't want innocent lives lost. Over the past few weeks, I'd gotten to know the people at our base, and I couldn't help imprinting each of their faces onto the bodies we'd found.

Isaac had moved away to catch up with Lorcan and Alex and run them through what was happening next. Kingsley had taken it upon himself to show George the helicopter, and they were both now standing with Jonathan. I was out of earshot, but the pilot pointed at the different parts of the aircraft, most likely telling the boy how each part worked to get the chopper into the air.

A figure appeared at my side, making me jump. Then I realized it was only Clay. He bumped me with his shoulder.

"You okay, sugar?"

Unexpected tears filled my eyes, and I blinked them back, glancing away, not wanting him or anyone else to see I'd been affected by what we'd found. I wanted to be as tough as the guys, to play my part alongside them. I didn't want them to see me as being weak.

I didn't want to look at him, so just nodded instead.

He stepped in closer and his fingers caught my jaw, gently drawing my face back around to his, and his thumb gently brushed away the tear that had escaped my eye.

"Hey, you don't have to hide how you feel from us," he told me.

"I just keep thinking about those kids," I admitted. "As if life hadn't dealt them enough blows, now they're in Hollan's hands. I wish we had done more. I wish *I* had done more."

"If this is too hard, you can always say you want out. None of us would think any less of you. We're all pretty damned impressed with everything you've done so far, but you weren't raised for this life. It's okay to say when it's too much."

I shook my head. "If I'm here with all of you, then nothing will ever be too much. My old life doesn't exist anymore. I can never go back to being that person I was before I met you. What would be the point? I'd rather die, knowing I had you, and Isaac, Kingsley, Lorcan, and Alex, than live the rest of my life without you all."

"Hey, no one's dying."

I wished he could say that for sure.

He put his arm around my shoulders, and together we joined the others.

Jonathan already had the helicopter warming up at Clay's request.

Isaac told him our plans, and the pilot's lips twisted. "I hate to be the bearer of bad news, but that could be a problem."

My stomach sank.

Isaac frowned. "Why?"

"I'm gonna have to refuel. We already used most of the fuel getting here. I have maybe another hundred miles' worth, but that's it."

"Shit."

"Okay," I started to calculate, the numbers jumping up in my vision, "if we both have to travel five hundred miles, approximately, and on the road they'll be covering eighty miles per hour, at the most, it's going to take them at least seven hours, and that's without taking into account any stops for fuel or rest breaks. It's going to take us less than half that time—three hours, tops. They're two hours ahead of us, but that still gives us a couple of hours to stop somewhere and refuel."

"She's right," Alex said, nodding.

Isaac turned to Jonathan. "How long is it going to take to refuel, and are we going to need to veer much off course to do so?"

The pilot shook his head. "No, it won't take long. We should still make it."

"Okay, but it's going to be tight. We can't waste any more time."

"What are we going to do about the kid?" Kingsley asked under his breath.

Isaac pressed his lips together. "We don't have time to do anything with him. I hate to say it, but he's going to have to come with us."

I agreed. "It's not ideal, I know, but we don't have any choice. If we try to divert to drop him off somewhere else, Hollan will beat us there. Besides, he's probably safer with us right now than anywhere else."

Kingsley turned to George with a grin. "You ready to take a ride, kiddo?"

The boy did a fist pump. "Yeah!"

He might have just witnessed the deaths of the men who'd been training him, and watched his friends being kidnapped, but he was still seven years old and excited about a ride on a helicopter.

The innocence of it kind of broke my heart.

Chapter Seven

Back on board, the rotor blades spun faster until the chopper lifted into the air.

It still felt unnerving to me, my stomach lurching, my fists tightening into balls. I was aware we had a child with us now, however, so I masked my nervousness with a smile.

"Fun, huh?" I said, though my voice was too high pitched, and I didn't think I was fooling anyone.

George looked equally unsure now we were actually in the air, but he returned my smile and nodded briskly.

I knew how he felt.

I couldn't stop myself thinking about the four boys who had been taken by Hollan. I thought of the men in their protective gear with their guns and the black vans. I imagined Hollan's men shoving them from behind, maybe even hitting them with the butts of their guns, forcing them to move when they were scared and maybe even crying. Or would the older ones have been defiant, remembering what they were being trained for? That defiance may have only earned them more violence, and I prayed none of them had been badly hurt.

Beneath us, we left the lake far behind, until it became only a shade of blue on the horizon. Green dots of bushes and trees blended together to become a patchwork of hues, divided only by the strips of roads winding between them. I had the strange thought that we were the only ones left, circling above the rest of the world like survivors of an apocalypse.

I leaned across Lorcan to stare down at the roads, and any tiny dots of vehicles made my heart lurch. Could they be Hollan? It was impossible to tell from this high up—they were nothing more than ants—and I knew Hollan would be way ahead of us by now. Hell, they might not even be taking the same route; it wasn't as though we had to worry about following the highways. Plus, we'd agreed we weren't going to try to take out Hollan that way, and we needed to wait until we'd told the next base of their impending arrival. Still, it didn't stop me imagining them below us, and how good it would feel to swoop down and shoot the bastards off the road.

I also realized we didn't know which vehicle the boys were being held in, and just shooting the vans off the road would also mean putting the lives of the boys in danger.

There was a different atmosphere in the chopper now. Where before we'd been tense but hopeful, now it felt as though we'd already failed. There were another four bases we still needed to reach, but now the reality that we might not win this thing sat heavy on each of our shoulders.

We were playing a game of chess, each of us trying to anticipate the other person's move before they made it. I wished we had some idea of how many men Hollan had been able to get behind him. If it was only a handful, we were on an equal footing, but if he had hundreds he'd been able to mobilize, then we'd already lost before we'd barely gotten started.

Up front, the pilot used the radio to call ahead and let whoever owned the place where we'd be refueling know we were coming. I guessed you couldn't just land and help yourself.

It felt as though we'd barely been in the air when the helicopter began to descend again. I looked down to see the gray strip of an airfield below us. The roofs of a couple of buildings were positioned at the far end.

"This is where we're going to refuel, folks," Jonathan said through our headphone sets. "Probably going to be a good thirty minutes, so you might as well use the time to stretch your legs. It'll be a couple of hours before you get to do so again."

I looked over to the guys. They wore similar expressions—jaws tensed, shoulders back. There had been a distinct lack of conversation, and when there was some, it was stilted and abrupt. I didn't like seeing the usual easy camaraderie between the guys being eaten away by regret and self-doubt. I knew all the worries going through my head would be going through theirs, too.

The helicopter grew lower in the sky, until I was able to make out the detail of the ground below. A large tanker was set to one side of the airstrip, a little way from the buildings. As I watched, a figure exited one of the buildings, and then stood looking up at us, his hand cupped over his eyes to shelter from the glare of the sun. I hoped this was someone we could trust, but I'd been having a hard time trusting anyone lately.

Jonathan didn't seem to be bothered by the person's appearance, as he continued to descend. I did, however, notice Lorcan's hand slipping down to where his gun rested in its holster at his hip. I had my own weapon on me, too. Now was not a time for letting down our guard.

The helicopter touched the ground with a couple of bumps, but then came to rest. The engine died around us, and the wop-wop of the blades began to slow. I tugged the headphones off my head and twisted to put them back on the hook on the seat behind me. Jonathan had already jumped out, and he opened the door for us to exit.

Lorcan led the way, and I followed. Kingsley helped George climb out, and we all stayed low as we moved away from the still circling helicopter blades, into an area of safety.

The figure I'd noticed before came forward. He was a man in his late fifties, with a belly straining against the buttons of his checked shirt, and jeans that looked as though they'd seen better days.

"I take it you're the folks who need to refuel," he called out, tipping the peak of the baseball cap he wore which had the blue 'A' insignia of the *Atlanta Braves* on the front.

Jonathan stepped forward. "Yes, sir." He shook the other man's hand. "Thanks for helping out."

"If you've got the money, I've got the fuel. Ain't nothing in this life comes for free."

"Absolutely. I assume cash is all right."

"Cash will work just fine."

Perhaps assuming we might need to talk, Jonathan jerked his chin toward George. "You ever seen a helicopter get refueled?"

The boy's blue eyes lit up. "No, sir!"

"Then today's your lucky day."

A wide smile broke out across the boy's face, and his hands clenched into fists. I was pretty sure he was stopping himself jumping up and down with excitement. At some point, he'd figure today was far from his luckiest day ever, having watched men he'd known get shot down in front of him, and having his future team members abducted, but for the moment he was caught up in the excitement of a seven-year-old boy getting to do something with a helicopter.

With George occupied, the rest of us wandered away from the chopper and onto the grass verge which ran alongside the runway. A couple of small planes sat outside one of the buildings I'd seen from the sky, but which I now saw was a hangar. I wondered if they belonged to the same man Jonathan had paid for the fuel.

"This won't take long," Isaac said, both hands shoved into the pockets of his suit pants as we meandered along, our pace belying the rush we were in. I knew he was trying to make us all feel better, but it didn't help.

"Shame we have to do it at all," Lorcan commented.

"Nothing we can do about it. We can't fly on air," said Kingsley.

"We're flying *in* air," I pointed out, my crappy attempt at a joke eliciting a weak smile from the guys.

Clay nudged me in the side with his elbow. "Boom boom."

I smiled back at him, and resisted the urge to snuggle in closer, to have him hook his arm around my neck in that way he liked to do, and let me lean in against his side. I wanted the support right now, but I guessed they all felt that way.

Something had been playing on my mind, and I couldn't shake it. I made sure George was out of earshot—the boy was fascinated with the refueling of the helicopter—before I spoke.

"Why do you think Hollan took the boys rather than killing them?"

Isaac pressed his lips together and shook his head. "I have no idea. Maybe he has a heart, after all."

Of all the reasons, I thought that was the least likely. "I don't think so. Hollan doesn't do anything out of emotion."

Another thing occurred to me. Hollan knew nothing about how these secret bases operated. He knew they existed, and he knew the men who came after people like him—corrupt people—were trained to do so, but he didn't know they had been raised their whole lives for the job.

"Maybe he wasn't expecting them to be there," I suggested. "If he doesn't know you guys are raised from childhood, and that you're all orphans brought into the system, he wouldn't have been expecting to find children there. Maybe that threw him, and he needed to know more, which is why he took them rather than killing them on the spot."

"She's got a point," Clay said, nodding.

Isaac rubbed his hand over his mouth, thinking. "So he took them to learn more about how we operate."

Alex looked between us. "Maybe to prevent any new bases springing up out of the ashes of the ones he knows about?"

"So he has taken them for questioning?" Lorcan asked.

Isaac dropped his hand from his mouth. "That would make the most sense."

I remembered how it had been when they'd wanted information out of me, the lengths he had gone to. I prayed he wouldn't hurt the boys in the same way. I said their names in my mind—T*ad, Scott, Xander, Chris.* I didn't know their faces, but I knew that much.

"I'm going to see if the old guy's got a restroom I can use," I said. I could use a drink and something to eat, too, but it didn't exactly look like there was a restaurant around here, and we didn't have time to sit and eat. I felt as though I was being selfish, too, thinking about my own needs when there were far more important issues to deal with.

The older man, the pilot, and George were all standing around the helicopter. A large hose and a nozzle led from the tanker, and was feeding fuel into tanks at the top of the aircraft. The acrid scent of a combination of diesel and aviation fuel filled the air, making my eyes water. They saw me looking over, and the older guy lifted a hand in a wave.

"I'm just looking for your bathroom?" I called.

"Back of the hangar," he shouted back. "It's not the prettiest of things. We don't get many ladies around here."

I threw him a grin. "Don't worry. I'm not much of a lady."

I left them to it and went in the direction he'd pointed out. At the front of the hangar, to the left, I noted a vending machine, which gave out soda and snacks for a fee. I didn't have any money, but I hoped the guys did. I still felt guilty about thinking of my stomach when lives were in danger, but the men were bigger than I was, and burned more calories, so I figured I probably wasn't the only one who'd be pleased to see the vending machine.

After I used the bathroom—which was as bad as the older guy had warned—I came out, drying my hands on a piece of tissue, to discover Clay and Lorcan had both found the vending machine for themselves.

"You know that shit will kill you," I said from behind them.

Clay glanced over his shoulder through the curtain of his hair. "It can line up and wait its turn, then."

He threw me a can of soda and a packet of chips. I snagged them out of the air, pleased I'd managed to catch them using my other hand, rather than let them fall on the floor. I was cautious catching things with my bad hand, though, aware that just the slightest knock could throw my fingers out of joint again.

The soda was cold, and I snapped open the ring pull and took a couple of gulps, the bubbles going up the back of my nose and making my eyes water. There wasn't much nutritional value to be had in the snacks, but the caffeine and sugar would keep me going for the moment.

Clay bought a couple of extra candy bars and started stuffing his jeans pockets.

"You hungry?" I quipped.

He looked back at me again. "Thought the kid might appreciate them."

"Good idea."

A part of me wished we could leave George here. I didn't like the idea that we were taking him from one death trap straight into another. But we didn't have time to take him somewhere safe, and it wasn't as though we could abandon him with a complete stranger. Besides, there might be a chance he'd remember something else that could help us. It was a long shot, but there was always the possibility.

"We're all done, folks!" the guy who owned the hangar called out. Money exchanged hands, and I wondered how many times we'd need to do this before this whole thing was over. Would it ever be over? Hadn't I bought into this life? I hadn't signed up for an easy life of early nights and Netflix on the TV. I was a part of this now, a life of never knowing what the next assignment would be, or what direction danger was coming from. I wanted to be with the guys so badly, but was I giving up my chance at a life at the same time?

I pushed my fears aside. There wasn't time for self-doubt now. There were children in danger, and the man I hated most in the world was responsible. I would see this through to the end, even if it might mean giving up my own life.

Clay, apparently pleased with his stash of junk food, left to join the others. I watched his walk, the way he swaggered side to side, so easygoing. He looked as though he was joining some buddies at the bar, rather than joining a group of spies to take down a corrupt, murdering, kidnapping son of a bitch.

A leather-jacketed shoulder nudged mine, and I glanced over to see Lorcan's serious dark eyes studying my face.

"You okay, princess?" he asked, ducking his chin toward me.

I forced a smile. "Sure. And I thought I told you not to call me that. You should know by now that I'm as far away from 'princessy' as it's possible to get."

He ignored me, perhaps understanding I was trying to use humor to cover how I was really feeling. "You're allowed to not be okay. You've been through a lot, and we've all been prepared for this kind of thing our whole lives."

"Thanks. It makes me feel better knowing I have you guys with me."

We were hidden in the shadowy corner of the hangar, out of view from the others. Lorcan, all dark and broody, with his tats and his *don't-mess-with-me* attitude, always seemed to soften a little when he was around me. I sensed it about him now, something in his eyes changing, his shoulders relaxing. He lifted his hand and swept my hair away from my neck, and then his fingers lightly trailed up my neck to my jaw. I twisted my head so my lips met his fingers. His thumb drifted over my lower lip, tugging it slightly, and a sudden, unexpected surge of lust raced through me.

Our bodies crashed together, and suddenly we were kissing hard, his hands knotted in my hair, mine around the back of his neck, my fingers digging into the short, silky strands at his nape. Both of us knew this couldn't go anywhere—even though I could feel Lorcan's erection pressing hard against my stomach. But it wasn't as though he could push me up against the door of the hangar and take me here and now, however much we both might want it. There were too many people around, and while I was sure Isaac and the others would be happy to join us, I figured the pilot and the guy who owned the hangar might have questions. This was just a snatch in time, a reaffirmation of why we were doing all of this—because we wanted to live, and enjoy each other—not because we thought it would lead to sex. Anyway, we had far more important things we needed to be doing.

"Come on, you two," a deep voice I recognized as Kingsley's called to us from outside. "I'm not going to pretend like we don't know what you're doing in there."

Lorcan and I broke apart. Heat flushed my cheeks, and I could see Lorcan was equally affected. He gave me a shy smile that made my stomach do crazy things, and then reached down to the front of his jeans to readjust himself.

"You might have to give me a minute," he said, and I pressed my fingers to my lips to stop myself giggling. I felt better, though, somehow stronger in myself, as if, through his kiss, Lorcan had reenergized me.

Chapter Eight

I stepped out of the hangar to find all eyes on me. The heat in my face increased, and I had to hide an embarrassed smirk. Lorcan was noticeably absent behind me, as he waited to avoid making it quite so obvious to everyone exactly what we were doing.

The hose that had been feeding the helicopter's tanks had now been withdrawn, so I figured we were good to go.

Lorcan emerged, his head down, both hands shoved into the pockets of his jeans. If it hadn't been for the presence of George, I figured the others would be ribbing him by now, but instead all he got was a couple of knowing glances.

"You guys ready?" Jonathan asked.

Isaac nodded. "Sure. We don't exactly have time to waste."

I didn't know if that was a jibe at me and Lorcan, but I felt it anyway.

Clay had given George the candy and soda, and the boy was happily filling himself full of sugar. I figured all this would hit him later. For the moment, he was getting helicopter rides and unlimited treats, but, depending on what happened, and whether or not we'd be able to get his friends back, things would crash down on him sooner or later. It wasn't as though he'd be able to go back to his old life either. The men training him were dead, and the location of the base had been revealed. I didn't know what was going to happen to him, or to any of the rest of us, for that matter. Would Hollan have passed the information on to others? He must have, for so many men to show up. And if the locations had been revealed, didn't that mean everyone would have to relocate? Assuming everyone survived. When this was over, everything would have to change, anyway, and I wondered where that would leave us all.

One by one, we climbed back on board and took the same seats as before. I finished my soda, but still had the snacks. I'd eat one and save the other for later. We had a couple of hours left to fly, and even though I knew we were heading into danger, that didn't stop the sitting here waiting part from getting boring. You could only look at the scenery for so long.

Above our heads, the rotor blades of the helicopter began to spin, and the engine grew louder. I'd always thought it was the blades that made a helicopter so loud, but I discovered it was the engine. Still, it didn't seem as loud as before, so I forewent the headphones for the moment, content just to sit.

The aircraft lifted into the air, and my stomach did that lurch that went with leaving it several feet below. The hangar and aircraft below us grew smaller as we put more distance between us, and I spotted the tiny figure of the man lifting his hand in a wave.

George peered out the window and waved in return.

The chopper reached a cruising altitude. I sat back in my seat and tried to relax the best I could. It wasn't easy, though, not when I knew what was to come. Feeling restless, I leaned forward to see Isaac with his laptop open in his lap. Knowing he wouldn't be able to hear me if I yelled, I lifted the headphones and slipped them over my head to talk.

"What are you looking at?" I asked, nodding to the computer.

"Satellite imagery of the next set of coordinates. The weather is being kind to us this time." He twisted the computer around so I could see the screen. It didn't look unlike the scenery passing below us now—just a patchwork of greens with a few roads traversing across it.

I wrinkled my nose. "Doesn't look like much."

"I've increased the area to keep an eye on anything suspicious that might be approaching. We're still hoping we get there before Hollan, but I figure this will allow us to potentially spot them if they're nearby."

"If we're nowhere close, we won't be able to do anything about it, though." I was feeling frustrated.

He shook his head. "But it will let us know what to expect when we get there."

More bodies. More missing children.

And at some point, assuming Hollan continued to take the boys when he moved from base to base, he'd run out of room for them in the vehicles he was traveling in. Then he'd have no choice but to kill them.

"How big do you think the next base is going to be?" I asked Isaac. "The last one was noticeably smaller than ours."

He shook his head. "No idea. I'd always assumed they were each around the same size, training the same number of youngsters to come up through the ranks, but it looked like the last one only had one generation they were bringing up. They must already have an adult team working out of there, or at least they had."

George spoke up, his voice muffled around the mouthful of Snickers he'd already stuffed in.

"They're the ones who teach us." His voice cracked. "I mean, the ones who used to teach us."

I put out a hand and squeezed the boy's shoulder, trying to offer him some kind of comfort. "How long had you been at the base?" I asked him.

He shrugged. "About a year, I guess."

"Where did you come from?"

"A boys' home in Atlanta."

"And there's something in particular you like doing, huh?" I asked, remembering how this all worked.

He perked up again. "Yeah, I love engines. Anything with oil!"

I glanced over at Clay, who was our engines guy, and he threw me a wink.

I sat back in my seat again. We still had another ninety minutes before we reached our destination. The temptation to grab Isaac's laptop and watch the area we were heading for, keeping an eye out for any sign of black vans, was strong, but I held myself back. That was Isaac's job, and he'd speak up the moment he saw anything. We should have overtaken Hollan by now, and would get there first. Unless he'd switched modes of transport, which I thought was unlikely, though I knew he did have access to a helicopter. But he wouldn't bother arriving there with only him and a handful of men. He was arriving to declare war, and he wouldn't do that without an army behind him.

Half an hour or so had passed. Unable to contain myself any longer, I leaned back to peer at Isaac's laptop again. "Any change?"

"Nope."

We still had about one hundred and sixty miles to go. Hollan and his vehicles might still have the same distance to travel, but we'd cover the same distance twice as fast.

I peered out the window. I knew I wouldn't see a snake of black vans winding along the highway, but that didn't stop me looking.

"Any idea where this base is going to be situated yet?" Alex asked from behind me.

Isaac pursed his lips, and I tried not to think about kissing him. "As you know, the coordinates aren't precise enough to give us an exact location, but there is a small cluster of houses on that spot."

Alex frowned. "You think a base would be located near civilian homes?"

"That's what's throwing me, too," he replied. "Too many people would ask questions if they saw people coming and going from a building—in particular if all those people were men—and they didn't know the reason for it. My guess is it's somewhere on the outskirts, but I haven't figured out where yet."

"They're going to notice a helicopter of this size landing, and then it's going to get even more attention if Hollan arrives in his convoy and people start shooting."

Isaac ran his finger across his lips. "Yeah, I have thought of that. There must be something I'm missing."

"So let someone else take a look." Alex held out his hands for the computer, and Isaac handed it over.

Alex studied the screen for a while, his face pinched as he concentrated.

"What's that?" he asked eventually, tapping the screen. He held the laptop out so the rest of us could see.

Isaac frowned. "Looks like a facility of some kind, but it's not on any of the maps."

"What's that beside it?" Kingsley pointed to the screen as well.

Alex's lips twisted. "As far as I can tell, it's a farm."

"That doesn't seem odd to you?"

He nodded, clearly understanding what Alex was getting at.

"You think that might be our place?"

"Possibly. Some kind of facility, in a field, next door to a farm, which isn't even showing on a map. I'd say that's enough to go on."

Kingsley leaned over and jabbed at the screen again. "Looks like there's a satellite for communications in the grounds, too."

Isaac looked between us all. "I think we have our base."

"And there's still no sign of Hollan's convoy?" I asked, anxiety buzzing through my veins.

Isaac shook his head. "Nope, but remember we didn't spot anyone the last time, and that was because we were too late."

I pictured all the bodies we'd found, and a shudder ran through me. I didn't want to think about what we'd do if we came across the same thing again. It would feel as though everything had been for nothing.

Isaac left the laptop with Alex and leaned toward the front of the helicopter to get the pilot's attention. The noise of the aircraft was much louder up front, and I knew he would be grateful for the headset. He used it now to speak to Jonathan.

"You need to set us down near the big concrete building over there, the one with the satellite dish in its grounds. We think that's our place."

Jonathan nodded. "Roger that."

Right away, the helicopter banked to the right, and my fingers tightened around the edges of my seat, my muscles tensed as I held on. Even though I knew I wasn't going to fall out, instinct made me react. The helicopter lost height quickly and left my stomach right up there with it. I didn't want to look at how quickly we were approaching, but it was like a car crash, and I couldn't quite help but look.

The gray of the concrete building rose, the white circle of the satellite dish growing bigger, catching the glare of the sunlight. It did look out of place among the barns of the adjacent farm and the green of the surrounding countryside. Farther down the road was a small cluster of houses. I wondered what the people who lived there thought of this place. Did they gossip about it and make up stories, thinking it was some top secret government facility, or had they just accepted it into the scenery of their lives, and thought it was some kind of processing plant or something?

We landed hard in front of the building, and the helicopter blades began to slow.

For the second time today, I was painfully aware of how the last thing we were doing was making a quiet entrance. Every inhabitant of the hamlet nearby, and the farm the potential base was next to, would be twitching their curtains, wondering why this huge helicopter was landing in the field beside them.

Lorcan leaned over and opened the helicopter door from the inside. We all climbed out, caught between wanting to stretch out muscles that had been cramped into the same spot for so long, and watching out for signs that we might be attacked at any moment. We hadn't seen any indication of Hollan's convoy from the air, but that didn't mean they weren't here.

Jonathan climbed out as well, and George followed us.

"Can the boy stay here with you?" Isaac asked Jonathan. "It might be safer for him."

George's face crumpled. "No, I want to come with you!"

But Isaac stood firm, ignoring George's plea and continuing to address the pilot. "If you see anyone approach, in particular if they're driving black vehicles, don't wait for us. Just get the chopper into the sky and put some distance between you and this place."

Jonathan frowned. "What if you need to make a getaway?"

"We'll signal you. Don't go so far that you lose sight of the area."

He gave a brisk nod. "Roger that."

I didn't know how we were going to get inside. There hadn't been any sign of anyone yet, and even the farm beside it had remained quiet. In fact, it was too quiet. If this was a regular business, people would have appeared by now.

I was, however, relieved to see the heavy metal double doors of the main entrance remained shut. That was a good sign. At the Atlanta base, we'd found the door ajar.

"They don't know we're coming," I said, "so how are we going to get them to trust us enough to let us in?"

Isaac looked to me. "They'll have cameras all over this place, assuming we're in the right spot. Devlin gave me something for this precise reason."

I was glad to see Isaac had things under control. He was a good person to have around.

He reached into the inside of his jacket pocket and pulled something out. It looked like a leather wallet, only thinner. He flipped the item open and held it up into the air. Curious, I peeped around. A gold badge I didn't recognize made up the top half, and an ID card was on the bottom. He held it above his head and stepped closer to the building. He turned slowly, showing it to any hidden cameras that might be around to let whoever was manning them know that we were part of them. The helicopter continued to thrum, ready to sweep us out of there if need be.

A voice suddenly sounded from a speaker embedded into the wall, making me jump. "State your purpose."

Isaac took a step closer. "We're from the *Ghost Agency*. We need to speak with whoever is in charge."

Ghost Agency. I'd never heard them call it that before. That must have been the name Devlin had given to Isaac to prove who we were. It occurred to me that I had probably only scratched the surface about what these people did.

There was a pause, and my gaze scanned the front of the building, trying to get an idea where we were being watched from or if someone would materialize. Then something made a loud click, and the main door cracked open.

Chapter Nine

I exchanged a glance with the guys, and Isaac nodded, silently telling us it was okay to proceed. He led the way, Lorcan following, with me next, and Kingsley and Alex bringing up the rear.

We'd stepped into an industrial looking building, with concrete walls and a tiled floor underfoot. And we weren't alone.

Three people were waiting for us inside the entrance. Two were men, both dressed casually in jeans and polo shirts, and, to my surprise, the third was a woman. She was tall, in her forties, I guessed, with short dark hair, and wearing a navy blue pants suit. I experienced a ridiculous stab of jealousy at my men all being faced with someone who was clearly a leader of their team, and not only that, sharp, sophisticated, and beautiful. I suddenly felt ridiculously young and scruffy in my jeans and t-shirt.

She nodded to us, and then stepped forward, leaving the men a pace behind. Before she'd even said anything, it was clear she was the one in charge. The two men gave the impression of being little more than bodyguards, and I noticed both of them were armed.

"It's been a long time since we've been contacted by other *Ghosts*," she said.

"I'm Isaac." Isaac stepped forward to meet her, his hand out. "I head up the team from the D.C. base."

I noticed how they only ever used first names. Again, I'd never thought to question this. Did they have surnames, or were those taken from them at the same time they moved into the bases?

She took his hand and they shook briefly. I knew the woman's grip would have been as strong as Isaac's.

"My name is Andrea, and I lead this base." Her gaze shifted to me, and a muscle flickered beside her right eye. "You have a woman on your team?"

I sensed the others close in around me—barely a perceptible movement, but just a fraction, enough to let me know they were protecting me.

"Darcy here has some unusual abilities," Isaac said. "She's played an important part in recent events. Our base leader believed she would be an asset to our team."

Andrea flashed me a smile, and I felt bad for thinking not-so-nice thoughts about her a moment before. "I'm sure she is. Welcome, Darcy."

I ducked my head. "Thanks."

Andrea's lips thinned as she moved back to business. "I'd say I was pleased to meet you all, but I'm assuming you're not here with good news."

Isaac shook his head. "Sorry, but we're not. The locations of each of the training bases have been compromised, and I'm afraid they haven't fallen into the right hands. A man called Lyle Hollan is an FBI agent who's been working under the radar for many years. He's aware of us, and what we do, and he's the one who has the coordinates for each of the bases."

Andrea frowned. "What does he plan on doing?"

"He's not planning. He's already putting things into action. We just left the Atlanta base, and everyone there is dead."

Horror crossed her face. "Everyone? Jesus Christ."

"Not the boys. He's taken the boys, though we're not sure why. We believe it might be to learn more about how we work for future reference. Prior to this, he only knew there were training bases. He didn't know how we train our spies from childhood."

"What happens to us if the locations of all of the bases have been compromised? Where are we supposed to go?"

Isaac shook his head. "I don't know."

"This is the exact reason no one person was ever supposed to know all of the locations. How did it even get out?"

Guilt burned through me, turning my face hot, and making me wish I could sink into the ground and vanish. I sensed Isaac look at me, but I couldn't meet his eye. I was the one who'd given up the code to Hollan. I was responsible for all of this. If I'd only let him kill me, then yes, maybe the bases would never be able to contact each other again, but at least they'd all be safe.

"The locations were all on a memory stick," Isaac said, "and the memory stick fell into the wrong hands."

Her face became hard planes of anger. "Who would do something so stupid?"

"There's no point in slinging mud around now," said Kingsley. "We're running out of time, and standing around talking isn't going to help anyone."

Andrea paused and glanced away, studying the floor with concentration, though clearly thinking about all the information she'd just been given. Finally, she looked up again and refocused on Isaac.

"I'm not trying to question you, but please understand that I've never met you before, and now I'm just supposed to take your word that all of this is true?"

Isaac nodded. "It's a big ask, I know, but I wouldn't even know where this place was located unless I'd had access to the coordinates."

She lifted a hand to stop him. "I thought you said this other man, the FBI agent, had the memory stick."

"He does, but Darcy is good with numbers. She was able to memorize each of the coordinates before he downloaded them and made his escape."

The older woman's eyebrows lifted. "That's a lot of numbers to remember."

"I told you she was an important member of our team." He flicked a small smile over to me, and my cheeks heated. "Anyway," he said, turning his attention back to Andrea, "I have other proof. When we were at the Atlanta base, I downloaded the security footage onto my laptop. I can show it to you, so you can see what you're potentially dealing with."

Isaac reached into the bag he had strapped across his body and pulled out his slim line laptop. Balancing it in one hand, he fired up the machine and then tapped the keys one-handed. I almost didn't want to look at the screen, knowing I was going to see a replay of Hollan's men jumping out of the vans, of people falling as they were shot, of the same men stepping over the bodies, uncaring for the lives they'd just taken. A part of me felt as though I was looking into the future, as though that could be us in less than an hour's time. The idea made my chest tighten, my lungs constricting the air, and I had to look away to be able to breathe again.

Andrea watched with her hand clamped to her mouth. I noted that despite her outwardly groomed, cool exterior, her nails were bitten down to the quick. I guessed she lost some sleep from her job role, too.

"You believe me now?" Isaac asked, snapping the lid of the laptop shut.

She nodded, her face pale. Even the color appeared to have leached from her lips. "Yes. Those poor people."

"I'm afraid there's worse news to come."

Her jaw tightened. "Tell me."

"We have reason to believe they're coming here next."

Her shoulders stiffened in her suit jacket. "And they're planning to attack?"

"Yes, without a doubt."

Armed men had been waiting behind her, perhaps planning on starting to shoot should we turn out not to be who we said we were.

Andrea turned to them now. "Go, set the alert." Both men nodded and ran off. She looked back to Isaac. "How much time do we have?"

"I believe we're maybe an hour ahead of Hollan, but that could be less now. We need to get everyone prepared."

"How many men does he have?" she said, already turning to walk away, deeper into the building. Around our heads, an alarm began to sound, and lights in the walls started to pulse.

"We're not totally sure. But we saw four vehicles, each with perhaps six men inside."

"So, at least twenty."

"Yes, ma'am. How many do you have here?"

She shook her head. "Nowhere near that many. Six trainees. Four adults, including myself."

"Shit."

That meant there were half of us, compared to Hollan's troop.

"We need to move before they get here," Lorcan said. "We won't be able to hold out against them with those numbers."

"We've got the stronger hold," she replied. "They'll have to approach, and we can take them down as they do."

Lorcan's eyes narrowed. "You don't know this man. He's ruthless."

Her eyebrows lifted, her head tilting to one side. "So am I."

I joined the conversation. "What about the boys he's taken from the other base? He might use them as a way to get in here."

Andrea fixed me with a steely blue gaze. "Then we'll have to deal with that when it happens. We need to know when they're approaching. I've got some satellite equipment, but there's a delay."

"The chopper can go airborne again," Isaac interjected. "The pilot will let us know if anyone is coming."

Her eyebrows lifted. "You can trust him?"

Isaac nodded. "He's never given me any reason not to."

"Okay, do it."

I wasn't sure what the plan was yet. Were we staying here to fight, or were we going to run? I didn't know which would be better. I didn't like the idea of fighting *or* running. If we ran, it would leave Hollan open to continuing what he was doing, and we'd be abandoning those poor boys. But there were children here as well. Wouldn't we be putting them in danger if we chose to stay? It seemed like whatever ended up happening would be the wrong choice.

The men who'd been shadowing Andrea reappeared, waiting for their next orders.

"Is there anywhere your trainees can go that will be safe?" I asked.

"In the building?"

I thought of how George had hidden, and nodded.

She placed her fingers to her lips. "Maybe. There's a food storage cellar on the bottom level. They could hide in there."

"If they're somewhere safe," Lorcan said, lifting his chin, "the rest of us can position ourselves around the building, armed, and wait for Hollan to approach. You have windows here. I assume they open?"

Andrea nodded. "They're currently locked and armed with an alarm, but yes, they'll open if I switch it off."

"Good," he said.

"And switch off this alarm," Isaac said. "You'll alert anyone on the outside that something is wrong."

"The building is soundproofed," she responded. "No one knows anything about what goes on in here."

"Okay, but cut it anyway. It'll only make everyone anxious."

Andrea jerked her chin at the waiting men, and they turned and ran off, vanishing around a corner. A moment later, a blissful silence fell over the building. I didn't know how long it would last—I feared the sound of gunfire would soon take over—but for the moment it allowed us to breathe.

Some young faces appeared around the corner. They ranged in ages from around seven, right up to mid-teens. All were boys.

"What's happening?" the oldest one asked. He was tall and skinny with spiky dark hair and a turned-up nose. He glared at us, as though challenging us through a look alone.

Andrea wasn't going to sugarcoat things for them. After all, they'd been raised knowing what sort of job they'd be going into. "We believe some people might be coming here. Bad people. We'll deal with things, but in the meantime, we need you to all go down to the cellar and stay there until it's over."

The older boy, I guessed him to be in his mid-teens, straightened. "I want to fight, too. I'm old enough, and I'm the best shot out of anyone. I'm not going to hide away like some little kid."

Andrea huffed out air through her nose, her lips pressed together, and I could see she was considering what he'd said.

"We do need as many hands as possible," said Lorcan. "We're already outnumbered, two to one."

He must have been able to see himself in that young man's face. When he'd been that age, he wouldn't have wanted to hide either, but would have wanted to stand side by side with the other men with a weapon in his hand.

"Okay, Jared," said Andrea. "You can stay. The rest of you, I need you to go down to the dry store and stay in there, okay? I don't want you to come out unless one of us comes to get you, or unless everything goes quiet." I knew what she was talking about. If everything went quiet, it would mean that we'd lost, and when those boys came out of the dry store, all they would find would be our bodies.

"If you need to go for help," she continued, "you walk to the nearest house. Okay? But make sure there's no one else here first. If it's someone you don't recognize, none of these men, or this woman, standing here now, then hide until they're gone."

I realized she hadn't told them to go to the farm. Did that mean the place was empty, perhaps positioned purely to stop this facility from standing out so much?

"No, I don't want to go," cried one of the younger boys. "I want to stay here with you."

"Everything will be fine, but I need you guys out of the way, okay? These people have come here to help us, but there's something we have to deal with first."

I forced a smile. "Come on," I said to the boys, taking a few steps toward them. "How about you show me where it is? I bet we can find something good to eat in there while you're waiting."

The younger ones' faces relaxed at the promise of snacks.

One of the boys, about ten years old, scowled and folded his arms across his narrow chest. "I'm not a baby. I don't want to go down with them. If Jared gets to stay up here, I don't see why I can't."

"Jared is a lot older than you, Hudson," Andrea snapped. "Besides," her tone softened, "the younger ones are going to need someone older to look out for them, and you're our best bet right now. Can you do that? Be in charge of the younger ones while we're trying to work things out up here."

Hudson's shoulders relaxed slightly, and he glanced over at the other boys who were all standing back, one of them with his arm around the other's neck. I remembered how Isaac and the others had explained to me how they'd grown up together, how they saw each other as close to siblings as it was possible to get. I guessed these boys felt the same way, even though they might not be showing it right at this moment.

"Okay," Hudson reluctantly agreed.

"Thank you, Hudson," she said, though her voice betrayed no emotion.

I clapped my hands. "Why don't you guys show me where you're going? I'd like to see around." They each looked at me like I must be crazy for wanting to do such a thing, but I continued with the smile, only wanting to get them out of the way before the shooting started.

Alex stepped into line with me. "I'll come with you."

I glanced up at him with a grateful smile, admiring his profile for the briefest of moments. The long, dark blonde eyelashes. The little bump in his otherwise straight nose. The way his bottom lip was fuller than the top. I allowed myself a moment to appreciate how classically handsome he was—not perfect, by any means, but just the sort of well-groomed man who would catch any woman's eye.

The boys turned as a group to lead us through the building, and we followed. Hudson headed up the small gang of five; we'd left the older boy, Jared, with Andrea, Isaac, and the others.

The stairs leading down to the cellar were at the end of the corridor, twisting down into a spiral. Hudson led the way, the boys traipsing after. They were quiet, and I assumed this was out of character. The trainees back at our bases were always teasing each other about something, punching each other in the shoulder, or running everywhere rather than walking. They seemed to communicate through play-fighting—something I was sure I hadn't done when I was younger, and something I contributed to being the difference in the two sexes. These boys were sullen and nervous, and they clearly realized something was wrong. I doubted they got many visitors here, especially not in a relatively big group of six, like we were.

We reached the bottom level and continued along the corridor, so it would have brought us directly beneath where the others were standing. A number of doors led off the corridor, which were also used for storage, I assumed. The low ceiling, dank light, and the cold temperature made me hope the boys wouldn't have to spend long down here. I hoped we'd still be in the main part of the building with them when they eventually emerged.

"Here." Hudson stopped in front of one of the doors.

Alex reached past him to push the door open, and then reached in to flick on the light switch positioned on the wall just inside. White light flooded the place. It was exactly as Andrea had said, a dry store filled with goods. Metal shelves divided the room into several partitions, so it was impossible to see right to the back.

"You guys get behind here," I told them, gesturing to the back of the store room. "If anyone comes in who you don't recognize, you stay quiet, okay?"

"Who's coming to hurt us?" One of the youngest boys—who had blue eyes, blond hair, like Alex—added.

Alex stepped forward. "No one is coming to hurt you. They don't even know you exist, okay? It's this place they don't like, not you, but if we want them to go away and leave you alone, we're going to need you to stay super quiet, even when everything gets kind of loud and scary. Do you think you can do that?"

I didn't think anyone ever said no to Alex, and the boys all nodded obediently.

"Great. Now, let's see what snacks we've got in here to keep you busy in the meantime."

I was thankful to Alex for stepping in.

"There's chips on that shelf," one kid piped up, pointing at a shelf near Alex's head.

"Yeah, there's cookies there, too," said Hudson. "They put all that stuff there thinking we can't reach it, but we can just pull the stool over."

The boys laughed at their shared joke at getting one over on their trainers. Alex reached up and pulled a number of packets down from where they'd been pointing and threw them to the boys.

"There you go. That should keep you going for awhile. But don't come back up when they're finished. Wait until one of your trainers, or even one of us, comes down to get you. Got it?"

"Got it," the boys repeated in unison, their mouths already filled with junk.

Alex and I retraced our steps, closing the door behind us.

"I'm tempted to lock them in," I said, "but what if there's a fire of something?"

He shook his head. "Don't lock them in. It won't do any good. The lock's on the outside, so, if Hollan gets past us, he'll only unlock it again."

"I'm glad you're here, Alex."

He grabbed my hand and tugged me against him. "Hey, I'm glad you're here, too, though I hate that you're in danger."

"No more than the rest of you. And even when we're facing down armed men, I still feel safer with the five of you than I do any time when I'm on my own."

His body pressed against the length of mine. My hands were in both of his, and he straightened his arms, pulling me even closer, flush against his body. He ducked his head to press his forehead to the top of mine. He was so much taller than I was.

"You'll never be alone again, Darcy. Not with us around."

"There are quite a few of you," I admitted.

"You can handle us." His tone had become gravely. "I know you can."

"All of you." My voice was breathy in return.

"All of us."

He smelled so good, of aftershave and simply him, and I had to resist burying my face against his neck and pressing my lips against his skin. I wanted so badly to stay there with him, hide away a little longer, as I'd done with Lorcan in the hangar, but I knew there wasn't time.

"We'll continue this later." I said, forcing myself to release his hands.

I hoped we'd get a later.

Chapter Ten

We left the boys safely ensconced down in the cellar, and made our way back to ground level. Isaac and Andrea were standing side by side where we'd left them, and I pushed away a stupid rush of jealousy. It was a pointless emotion, and I had no right to be jealous, especially when I had a thing going with each of them and they'd never shown me a single glimpse of the green-eyed monster. But then they all knew and trusted each other, whereas this woman was a stranger to me, and I didn't want her moving in on my man. Or any of my men, for that matter.

Isaac spotted us over Andrea's shoulder. "Everything go okay?"

Alex nodded. "Yeah, we bribed them with snacks. Seems to work well on kids. Where are the others?"

"Checking out the rest of the building, and looking for the best vantage points. It's flat around here, so at least we'll spot Hollan long before he gets here."

"No sign yet?" I asked.

Isaac shook his head and rubbed his fingers over his lips. "Not yet, though they can't be too much longer. Unless something has caused them to stop, of course. They might have been held up by something."

"Let's hope they're permanently held up."

I didn't think there would be much chance of that happening. There wasn't much that seemed to get in Hollan's way.

"You should see the rest of the building, so you know your way around," said Andrea, already walking away. "We're all on this one level, with the exception of the cellar, which you've already seen. This place isn't as high-tech as some of the others, I believe, but we have everything we need."

"Any way of getting in touch with any of the other bases?" Isaac asked, and I detected the hint of hope in his voice.

"No, sorry. We've been in the dark as much as I imagine you've been over the last few years. We've worked with people locally, but I'm afraid we didn't know anything about the rest of you. We kept our ears to the ground, but never heard anything either." She offered me a small smile, as though she was pulling me in on a private joke. "That's the thing about spooks. We're not supposed to be noticed, not even by our own kind."

We continued down the corridor, our shoes squeaking on the tiled floor. This place had the feel of an old hospital—completely different than the high-tech place we'd left near D.C. Was this one of the early set-ups, or a more recent one? And why hadn't they put more money into it? I felt bad for the boys who lived here. I wouldn't want to be raised in this sterile place, miles away from anywhere. I knew most of the children's homes they'd been brought from probably weren't much better, but a part of me had hoped they'd be given more. I walked with Isaac on one side, and Alex on the other. I wondered where Kingsley, Clay, and Lorcan were. I didn't like us being separated. It made me anxious—even more so than normal.

"I expect the layout is much like you're used to," she said, and Isaac and I exchanged a glance. I knew he was thinking much the same as I was; this wasn't really anything like what we knew.

"Here." She opened the first door on our right, and I relaxed a fraction.

The room was wall to wall with computer screens. A man sat in front of them, monitoring them. He swiveled in his seat to half face us.

"Anything unusual yet, Matt?" she asked.

The man shook his head. "All still looking quiet, Andrea."

"Let me know the moment anything changes."

On one of the screens was the helicopter, still sitting outside, waiting for us. I noted the blades had stopped spinning. I hoped George was all right out there with the pilot. I knew he was happy being in the chopper, and Jonathan was probably keeping him entertained with helicopter facts, but a part of me wondered if we should have brought him inside to hide down in the cellar with the other boys. At least then he'd be with kids his own age.

The thought of the children automatically made me think of the boys Hollan had taken. Were they frightened, crying? Would Hollan get what he wanted from them, and then kill them? It seemed inhuman that he would do such a thing, but I didn't want to underestimate him. Would he do it just to get back at me, or was I putting too much importance on my existence? After all, he had what he wanted from me. Sure, I hadn't made things easy for him, but perhaps now he thought of me as merely an inconvenience, and of no importance at all.

Everyone moving on broke me from my thoughts, and I followed Andrea, Isaac, and Alex out of the room and back into the hospital-like corridor.

Again, this base looked far smaller than the one we'd left behind. Was our base the main one? It made sense, with its location being so close to D.C. The remaining two we had yet to visit didn't look as though they were close to any major cities. A twinge of unease plucked at my nerves. If we were the biggest base, wouldn't it make sense that ours was the one that should be targeted first? But then again, I had to remind myself, Hollan didn't have that information. Unless he looked at the locations of the bases, and decided that the one closest to D.C. would make the most obvious choice when it came to taking out the main one.

Devlin had been convinced Hollan wouldn't go there first because we knew he had all the locations, and we were ready for an attack. Devlin believed Hollan would want to take on the new locations, as they'd be unprepared and would be taken by surprise, and that was true of the Atlanta base.

Just as in the other bases, there was an industrial kitchen, though this one was slightly smaller than the others. The next room was a combined dining area and living space, with a long wooden dining table on one side of the room, and a U shaped corner of couches, together with a flat screen television, a games console, and a wall filled with shelves of books on the other. Cushions were positioned on the couch, and a thick rug covered part of the floor where the couches were located. Coffee cups and magazines were stacked on the coffee table. To my relief, this place suddenly looked a little less like the poor cousin. My worries about the boys being raised in a cold, unforgiving environment appeared unfounded.

We walked through several other rooms—the dormitory, which looked like the boys shared bunk beds, and a couple of separate rooms, which I assumed were where the adults slept. There were a couple of classrooms, one of which was clearly set up for science. There was no sports hall—the size of the building didn't accommodate it—but there was a well-equipped gym. I briefly wondered how the boys were taught to swim. Were they taken to a local pool?

"Can you guys swim?" I asked Alex as we walked.

He laughed. "Yeah, of course we can swim."

"But where, and how?"

"Darcy, no one notices a group of boys going into a swimming pool. And the people who raised us have enough sway to get private lessons, if needed."

"Right, of course."

I remembered what Devlin had always told me, how no one was a prisoner. The boys stayed because they were given a better standard of living than they previously had, and maybe the older ones realized they were also being given an opportunity that would never arise for them otherwise. But with the opportunity also came danger. Were they made aware of that side of things? That they were risking kidnapping and being shot at the same time? Or was it like anything when you're young, where you know of the dangers, but the possibility of it happening to you feels as unlikely as growing old?

Right now, I had four boys who'd been taken, and another five hiding downstairs in a cellar. Yes, they might grow into men like Isaac and Alex and Clay, but was the sacrifice worth it in the end? Shouldn't they just be allowed to be children, and grow into regular guys with regular jobs and families to come home to at the end of the day? Maybe people like Hollan and other men they'd dealt with over the years should just be allowed to get on with it, and the normal authorities should deal with them when they messed up. Maybe all of this simply wasn't worth it.

I experienced a pang of guilt at my thoughts. I'd agreed to come on board and be part of the team, so wasn't I as responsible for these children as anyone else who worked as ... what had Isaac called it? A ghost? And these children had been living peacefully enough until I'd opened my big mouth to that reporter all those weeks ago. It felt like a lifetime ago now. I was judging the way they worked, but I'd played my part.

'Cause this wasn't a normal tour. I could tell that by the way my heart was constantly in my throat, and I found myself jumping, my pulse racing, at every single sound. No, we were being shown the layout of the place so we would be better prepared when they came under attack. We needed to figure out the best places to put armed men, so we would be able to cover the entrances to the building.

We came across some of the others—the older boy, with one of the men who'd been guarding Andrea when we'd first arrived, and Kingsley and Clay. The windows of the room were frosted to prevent any curious eyes from peeping in, but a couple of them stood partially open now, with the men checking their vantage to the outside area, and making sure they had enough cover from the wall beside and under the window to take cover should Hollan's men start returning fire.

"We need to cover the back of the building, too," instructed Andrea.

"We're fighting with you," Isaac added. "Make sure you give us positions."

She nodded. "You know this man, so perhaps you'll be better at the front, with me. I don't know if there will be an opportunity to negotiate with him, but he'll probably respond to someone he knows more than a stranger."

Isaac's lips thinned, his nostrils flaring. "I'm not so sure about that. He's a man who takes action above conversation."

"He killed my father," I blurted, unsure where the words had come from. I certainly hadn't planned for them to come out. "I was there. He died in my arms."

The older woman looked to me with a new kind of respect and sympathy. "I'm sorry to hear that. Did it happen recently?"

I shook my head. "No, but I only recently found out he was responsible. I guess we've been out to get each other ever since." I realized I'd made it sound as though this was a battle between me and Hollan that I'd somehow gotten everyone else involved in. "I mean, the reason he killed my dad was to get the locations to these places. It was only when he discovered it was encrypted and that I was the only one who knew the code to unlock it that I got involved."

"I see," she said, but I wasn't sure she really understood.

We bumped into Lorcan, checking out the weapons in the range. It was a long space that ran along the far end of the building. I figured it was a good thing the building was soundproofed. People would start asking questions if they kept hearing gunfire coming from the place.

"Hey," he said. "Plenty of ammo in here. If nothing else, we'll be able to hold them off for a while."

"Then what?" Isaac asked.

He shrugged. "We hope for a miracle."

Chapter Eleven

Leaving them to strategize, I went downstairs and checked on the boys in the cellar. Two of them had fallen asleep, one of them with his head on ten-year-old Hudson's lap. The older boys had a small games console, which they sat bent over, only glancing up as I entered.

"Is it over?" one of them asked, keeping his voice down.

I still felt bad about them being down here. I knew it was safer—I didn't want them exposed when the shooting started—but it still felt callous.

I shook my head. "Sorry, it's not even started. I just wanted to see how you guys were doing."

Hudson shrugged. "We're okay. Just kinda bored."

"You've got your game, right? Who's winning?"

"Him." He jerked his head in the direction of the boy sitting beside him. "He always wins."

"No, I don't," the other boy protested. "And even if I do, it's only 'cause you don't pay attention and make stupid mistakes."

Sensing my presence was more likely to start a fight than anything else, and figuring they'd been perfectly happy left alone before I'd come in, I slowly backed out of the room and left them to it. I hoped they wouldn't be forced to stay down here much longer.

How long had it been since we'd arrived? A good hour must have passed. Chances were, Hollan and his men would be here at any moment.

The thought put wings under my feet and set my heart racing. I propelled myself back up the stairs, almost expecting to discover Hol-

86

Ian had already arrived. I rushed back to the front of the building to find Isaac and Andrea watching through the windows positioned either side of the heavy main doors. Both held semi-automatic guns at their sides, ready to start shooting the moment it was needed.

"Any sign?" I asked.

They both looked over their shoulders at me.

Isaac shook his head. "No, nothing yet."

I chewed on my lower lip, anxiety coursing through my veins. My gun was a welcome weight at my hip, but I dreaded the thought of ending up in a gunfight between us and Hollan's men. I'd seen the video footage of them arriving at the previous location several times now, and with their full body armor and helmets, with even their faces covered with clear shields, it wasn't going to be an easy job taking them down. They'd meant business.

"Don't you think they should be here by now?"

Isaac turned to face me fully and shrugged. "Anything could have happened. We only ever estimated the journey time. If they stopped somewhere for longer, or took a different route, it could easily make them later."

I knew he was talking sense, but the waiting was killing me. I couldn't just stand in one spot and wait. Besides, they still had a guy watching the satellite footage. If it looked like anyone was approaching who shouldn't be, we'd get an early warning. It wasn't foolproof—the moment we got any cloud cover, the satellite would be useless, same for when it got dark, which wouldn't be far off—but for the time being, it was reassuring to have.

Leaving Andrea and Isaac where they were, I went to pace around the rest of the building. I found Kingsley and Clay in the living area, both sitting on the floor on either side of the window, their weapons laid on the floor beside them. Both their faces lit up when they saw me.

"Hey, sugar," Clay said, patting the spot beside him. "You come to join us?"

I sighed, the air chuffing out from deep inside my lungs, and went to drop down beside him. I wouldn't be able to sit still for long. "I'm worried they're not here yet."

"Anything could have happened," he said, parroting Isaac, and I rolled my eyes.

His eyebrows lifted. "What?"

"That's exactly what Isaac said."

"Then Isaac is probably right."

I sighed again, my shoulders slumping. Leaning to one side, I pressed my cheek against the bulk of his shoulder. He lifted his arm and pulled me in for a squeeze before letting me go again. I wished we could have stayed that way, with me tucked in under his arm, and maybe even have shut my eyes for a few moments, but we were supposed to be colleagues, and cuddling up with each other in front of Andrea's men didn't exactly look professional. The idea that the other woman might be having a similar kind of relationship jumped into my head, and I suppressed a smile, despite my inner turmoil. She was a lucky woman if she did, but I guessed this kind of setup didn't happen on a regular basis.

"How long do you think we should give them?" I asked.

Kingsley leaned forward to look at me. "Until what?"

"Until they show up? I mean, we can't just sit here waiting indefinitely. We're going to need to make a decision at some point."

Kingsley frowned. "You think they're not coming?"

The moment he said the words, it was as though the truth hit me in the middle of my forehead. I clamped my hand over my mouth.

What if we were wrong all this time? What if Hollan had never intended for this to be his next location?

The walls suddenly felt as though they were closing in. I was sitting in a shrinking box. I wanted out of there, and the certainty that we'd made a horrible mistake began to bloom in my chest, a cancer that, once it had taken hold, was going to be impossible to carve out.

I clambered to my feet. "I need to find Isaac."

I left Kingsley and Clay staring after me as though I'd lost my mind, and ran back down the corridor, my shoes squeaking on the floor with every step. Isaac and Andrea were in the exact same spot, and they shot me matching baffled looks as I hurtled toward them.

"I think we should leave," I blurted between gasps for breath. "Just grab everyone and get the hell out of here."

Isaac frowned at me as though I'd gone crazy. Maybe I had. Maybe the pressure had all gotten too much and I'd finally cracked. "If we do that, we won't be able to face Hollan, and take him out once and for all. And what about the boys he's taken? Are you suggesting we abandon them to whatever he has in store?"

"But he should be here by now." I paced the floor, my fingers at my mouth, chewing my nails. In my vision, I could see a timeline, only, for once, it wasn't my own. No, it was the timeline Hollan would have used if he'd made it to this spot in the allocated amount of time. Only now it didn't end, but instead wrapped around my body to the right, vanishing behind me. It should have ended here, but it didn't.

The feeling that something wasn't quite right wouldn't leave.

"What if we got it wrong?" I said. "We relied on George overhearing that they had five hundred miles to go to the next base, but what if he heard it wrong, or they were talking about something else? It would be easy enough for a small, frightened child to be mistaken."

"You think they went to another base?"

I shook my head. "I don't know, but the longer we're waiting around here, the more I'm sure they're not coming."

Clay and Kingsley had followed me down the corridor and were now standing behind me. I glanced back to find them wearing equally concerned expressions. Perhaps something I'd said had finally gotten through to them.

"What if Hollan was aware that George was hiding?" said Kingsley, his expression serious. "What if he said that to throw us off the scent?"

I hadn't thought of that. "You think he set us up so we'd ask George if he heard anything, and he'd repeat what had been said? You think they went somewhere else completely?" My stomach was sinking.

"When was the last time you were in touch with the home base?" I asked Isaac.

He frowned. "Not long. Thirty minutes. I called Devlin to give him an update. He told us to be careful, but that we were doing the right thing."

"And everyone there was okay?"

"Yeah, fine. No action happening." His frown deepened. "You think Hollan might have gone there instead?"

"Devlin said he wouldn't because we'd have been prepared for him, where the other bases wouldn't, but what if this was all a ruse so they let down their guard?"

Fear flicked across Isaac's handsome face, and he reached into his jacket pocket and pulled out his cell phone. "I'll call again, let them know our suspicions. Even if we're wrong, it won't hurt for them to be a little more vigilant."

I thought back to the team of people we'd left at the base—the skeleton crew of surveillance and security. Then there were all the youngsters we'd left, together with Aunt Sarah. I remembered the suggestion I'd made to Devlin right before I'd left, about how I thought Sarah should go home. I didn't know what I wanted right now—for her to have left and be safe at home, or for her to be there protecting those kids. Fear dried the saliva in my mouth, coating my tongue with a thick, copper taste, like old pennies. We were too far away, and we'd left the base almost defenseless. We'd taken the vast amount of weapons and ammo, assuming that we were the ones who were going to need it.

"What do we do?" asked Andrea, perhaps sensing our indecision.

Isaac already had the phone pressed to his ear. He lifted his hand in a motion to tell her to wait. "Shit." He hung up. "Devlin isn't answering."

Pricks of tears plucked at the backs of my eyes. "There must be others we can try?"

Already, he'd pulled out his laptop. "I'll try to connect with them remotely. Send a message to their server and try to put out an alarm."

I put out my hand. "Give me your phone. I'll call my aunt."

"She's just got a regular phone. She'll never get a signal if she's in the base."

"No, but there's a chance she might not be there."

He frowned at me. "Then what can she do?"

"Go back and warn them." I realized I might be sending my aunt into a war zone.

He pressed his lips together. "If Devlin isn't answering, it might be too late."

The acid in my stomach curdled. I couldn't stand the thought that we'd just been sitting here, waiting, while Hollan was destroying everyone we loved back home.

Kingsley stepped in. "Even if Hollan has gone there, he might not even be able to get in," he pointed out. "It's not like these other buildings that are more obvious. You have to know what you're looking for."

Isaac nodded. "Maybe, but Hollan's a smart man. He knows how we work. There's a good chance he'll figure it out."

"But then won't someone need to let him in from the inside?" Clay said, shoving both hands into his jeans pockets.

Isaac's gaze flicked across us. "Maybe he has someone on the inside."

I stared at him. "You don't mean that?"

He shrugged. "Honestly, I don't know. I'm just trying to think of all the possibilities." He turned his attention back to his laptop and hit a number of keys. "Dammit. I can't make a connection with anyone online either. Something is definitely going down."

"What about the satellite feed?" Kingsley asked. "Maybe that will give us an idea of what's going on down there."

But Isaac shook his head. "I already tried it. They've got cloud cover. It's not thick, and it'll probably pass, but for the moment I can't see a damned thing."

I stared between them in alarm. "We need to go back. Now."

Isaac looked to Andrea. "I know this isn't easy, but there are still three bases that are unaware of our current situation. If we give you the remaining coordinates, are you able to send people to them and warn them?"

She nodded. "Yes, of course. What about the rest of us, and the boys? Should we stay here?"

"No, the location has been compromised. You need to put some distance between yourselves and this place. You got anywhere you can go?"

"Yes, I think so."

"Good."

"You have all my contact details now, and I have yours, so stay in touch, and let me know what's happening. Make sure the other bases understand that they can't stay there. Even if we manage to stop Hollan, we have to assume the locations have been revealed to too many people to try to contain." He shook his head. "The whole point of our operation is that it's covert, even among ourselves. That's all fallen apart now."

Something in my chest tightened. I hated to hear the dejection in his tone. This wasn't the strong, determined Isaac I knew. It almost sounded as though he'd already given up.

Chapter Twelve

With the decision made, the base erupted into movement. "Alert the rest of the team," Andrea told one of the armed men who always seemed to be shadowing her. "We're going to need supplies and weapons, and pack the basic necessities. We don't know when we're going to be coming back."

"Yes, ma'am," the man replied. "How long until we leave?"

"ASAP. Ten minutes at the most."

He nodded and took off down the corridor at a jog, passing the instructions over to anyone he came across.

"Where are Alex and Lorcan?" I asked, looking between Isaac, Kingsley, and Clay.

"They're at the rear of the building," Kingsley said. "I'll go and find them, let them know what's going on."

I watched Kingsley's back as he ran off in the same direction as the other man. My stomach twisted uneasily. I didn't like watching him leave, but we all needed to separate in order to bring us back together again.

Isaac spoke to Andrea, his fingers lightly touching her elbow. "I wish I could be sure about Hollan's whereabouts. We're assuming he's gone back to D.C., but there's a chance he hasn't. Make sure you stay alert, and be careful approaching the other bases, just in case."

Her expression was tense. "I will." I couldn't imagine what was going through the other woman's head right now. Though she appeared cool and calm on the outside, she'd effectively had her world blown apart in the last hour. I knew they were trained for this kind of thing, but this was all still one hell of an upheaval.

"Do you have enough transport to get everyone out of here?" Clay asked.

Andrea nodded. "Yes, we do."

Isaac glanced toward the front door, and then frowned as though he'd thought of something. "I'm going to need a favor."

She looked to him. "Name it."

"We have the boy from the other base still out in the helicopter with the pilot. Can we leave him with you? We don't know what we're going to be going back to, and I don't want to put him in the middle of another mess."

"Yes, of course."

"His name is George."

"We'll take care of him," she said. "He'll be fine."

A restrained smile flashed across Isaac's face. "Thank you."

I hoped I was right about Hollan not turning up here, and we weren't about to get a surprise while we were trying to get everyone on the move. We'd be exposed while we were moving between the buildings and the transport, and that would make us vulnerable. Everything felt like a trap right now, and I still half expected Hollan to spring out from somewhere.

"You need to give me the coordinates of the other three bases," Andrea reminded Isaac.

He nodded. "I'll send them to you now."

"We'll divide into two teams, but assuming the other locations are miles away, we're probably going to end up driving through the night. I'll send one of my men to a different place with the boys, so at least we'll know they're all safe."

Isaac ducked his head. "Thank you."

She gave him the same kind of smile he'd given her a moment ago—one filled with both commiserations and hope. "I hope you can get the trainees from the Atlanta base back safely from this man, too."

"Yeah, so do we," he said. "And stay in touch. This whole idea of us being independent from each other might have worked when no one had access to the locations, but the moment it fell into the wrong hands, it was all over."

She pressed her lips together and nodded. "This part may be over, but we'll reform and start anew."

"I hope you're right."

He put out his hand, and the two shook. I wondered if we'd ever see Andrea and the other boys again, and that feeling of not being able to breathe hit me once more. I wished we had an ability to transport ourselves through the ether and be back at our base, but frustratingly we still had several hours of travel ahead of us before we'd be back there. What would we find when we arrived? Would my hunch have been incorrect, and Hollan had stayed one step ahead of us yet again? Or would we return to find everyone in the base slaughtered, and Hollan grinning triumphantly. I'd always felt as though this thing was personal between me and Hollan, even though I'd known it was far bigger than a grudge.

Despite what Isaac had said, I tried my aunt's cell phone. As he'd predicted, it went straight to voicemail. I left a message anyway. There might be a chance she'd pick it up.

"Aunt Sarah, it's me. I need you to listen. We think Hollan might be on his way to our base, if he isn't there already. You need to tell Devlin, and get everyone out. The boys included. Especially the boys. Take them back to the house in the city, and you go with them as well. You'll be safe there. We're on our way."

Why hadn't we done that to start with? Yeah, maybe we thought it was safe, but it wasn't. We should have shipped all the children out of there the moment we knew the locations had been compromised.

I hung up and glanced over to see the others watching me. I shrugged. "No answer, just as we expected."

"I'm sure your aunt is fine," Clay offered, but I knew he was only saying it to make me feel better. He had no way of knowing that, and we both knew they were empty words. If Hollan was already at the base, there was a good chance no one was fine.

Feeling like a third wheel, I wanted to do something useful. "I'll go down and bring up the boys," I offered. I felt bad that they'd been down there at all, but at least now we were getting them away from this place. I just hoped wherever they ended up would be safer.

"I'll come with you," Clay said.

I gave him a grateful smile. "Thanks."

We moved quickly down to the cellar. The kids were much as I left them the first time. Sensing my need to hurry, their eyes widened in fear.

"Is it happening?" Hudson asked. "Are they here?"

"No, but we're going to get everyone out of here. We don't think they're coming, but we still need to move fast, okay?"

"Where are we going?" the boy asked as they all got to their feet and started to file out.

"Andrea knows somewhere safe for you all," I replied, knowing that was pretty vague, but unable to give them any more detail. It wasn't as though I knew for myself.

I pressed my hand to each of their shoulders as they passed by, trying to urge them to hurry. We traipsed in a line back down the low-ceilinged corridor and toward the stairwell. The boys knew where they were going, and Clay and I moved along with them, keeping them together. I didn't want one of them running off and losing them in this building now.

We reached the top of the stairs, and Clay pushed the door open, allowing them to pile out.

Hudson paused before exiting, looking between me and Clay. "When are we coming back?" he asked.

I pressed my lips together and shook my head. "I'm not sure."

One of the younger ones I thought was called Charlie, who looked to be about six years old, adorable with blond hair and brown eyes, looked up at us. "Can I get my toy?"

I pulled a face, feeling awkward. "No, I'm sorry, but there's no time for that. I think they're packing you some clothes, but I'm not sure about toys."

Charlie's face crumpled and he started to cry. My heart just about broke.

Clay put his hand out to the child. "Come on, let's get you out of here. We can get you a new toy as soon as you're safe."

"I don't want a new toy," Charlie managed between little hitching breaths. "I want that one."

"Stop being such a baby," Hudson snapped.

"He's not a baby!" one of the other boys yelled.

I didn't know how to handle this. I'd never been around kids. I tried to remember my reason for volunteering to do this part of the job. Had it been because I felt responsible for the boys now in Hollan's possession? Yes, it must have been. That didn't mean I was any better equipped to handle them, though.

Clay stopped and dropped to a crouch, his hand on the arm of the boy who was crying. "Hey, what does your toy look like?"

The boy sniffed and ran his hand across his nose, leaving a shiny trail across his skin. "He's a dinosaur."

"Okay, I'll run and get him. You do what Darcy here tells you, and I'll be back with it before you've even noticed I've gone."

Charlie's tears stopped almost miraculously. I gave Clay a grateful smile, and he threw me a wink before vanishing off in the opposite direction, heading toward the dorm rooms.

I got the boys up the rest of the stairs and into the main part of the building.

People had begun to gather at the entrance, and, to my relief, I spotted Lorcan and Alex among them. Kingsley must have found them and let them know what was going on.

"Jonathan's getting the helicopter warmed up," Isaac said, spotting me. "We'll be out of here in no time."

They pushed the front doors open and stepped outside. I tried not to feel exposed at the sudden space. There was still no sign of Hollan, and, as each minute passed, I became more and more certain my hunch he wasn't coming had been correct.

To my surprise, across the field where the farm was positioned, now several expensive looking vehicles drove out of the barns. The windows were blacked out, and even though they'd been kept in not so luxurious surroundings, driving in these cars would get them noticed.

"You'd think they'd have more inconspicuous vehicles," Lorcan said to me from the corner of his mouth.

I pulled a face. I would have thought so, too, but that was what they had, and there was nothing we could do about it. Besides, I didn't think the helicopter was exactly subtle.

Thinking of the chopper, I looked to where Jonathan was walking toward us, George at his side. The pilot's hand was on the boy's shoulder. George appeared both curious about all the new people and worried about what might happen next.

Kingsley stepped forward to meet them and ducked his head to bring himself more on George's level. "You need to go with the woman who heads up this base, okay? Her name is Andrea, and you can trust her. It's safer for you. We're going to go and get your friends back."

"I want to come with you!" he cried.

Kingsley shook his head. "Sorry, kiddo, but we have to make the choice for what is best for you. There are no negotiations. It's happening, okay?"

They'd been raised to look up to authority, and to take orders. I could see in the boy's face that he didn't want to go, saw how he looked longingly at the chopper.

"See ya, kid," said the pilot. He gave him a high five, and then pulled him into a quick hug.

George's face twisted. "Thanks for letting me ride in your helicopter."

"Hey, any time."

"Time to go," called Andrea from where she stood beside one of the cars.

They started piling into the vehicles. George looked warily at the other boys, who gave him nods and smiles of greeting. George returned their smiles with a shy one of his own. I couldn't imagine how he felt, being pushed into the company of a whole heap of people he'd never met before. This wasn't exactly the best circumstances for them to meet either.

The little blond boy, Charlie, resisted getting into the car and started to cry again. "I didn't get my toy!"

Shit, what had happened to Clay? Worry stabbed at me.

The man trying to get the boy into the car rolled his eyes at the fuss the child was creating.

I glanced back toward the entrance. To my relief, Clay came charging out, waving a plastic dinosaur in the air.

"Hey, wait up, kid! Is this the one you're after?"

"Seratops!" the boy declared, reaching for it.

Clay handed the toy over, and the boy kissed the toy's spiky little head. Despite the circumstances, I couldn't help smiling. Clay would make a good dad one day. The thought had pinged into my head, and my heart flipped. I couldn't allow myself to think that way, to think of us all with a future. How would it even work with us? What if one guy wanted to be a parent, and the others didn't? How would we even know whose baby it was? Maybe it wouldn't even matter. Maybe they'd be content to see the child as all of ours, and the kid would get five dads instead of one. I didn't know how it would work when we tried to explain things at parent-teacher meetings, but families were made up of all shapes and sizes these days.

"Darcy? Everything okay?"

I realized Alex had been talking to me, and I gave my head a slight shake, trying to dispel the image of us all as a family. Alex would be another one who'd make a great dad. He'd be fantastic with the teachers, too, would schmooze them into not asking too many questions. *No, stop that, Darcy,* I scolded myself. We might not even survive the next twelve hours. I couldn't be thinking about babies.

"Yeah, fine. Just too many thoughts going around my head." My cheeks heated, but I had no intention of telling him just what those thoughts were. Maybe, when this was over, we'd sit down and have a conversation about where this was going, but that time wasn't now.

The boys were divided between two of the vehicles, and then followed by the adults. Everyone was ready to go.

Andrea gave Isaac's hand a final shake, and bade farewell to the rest of us with a raise of her hand. "Good luck. I hope everyone stays safe."

Isaac nodded. "You, too. Keep in touch."

The drivers climbed behind the wheels, and then they were pulling out of the area.

I breathed a sigh. They were leaving, putting distance between themselves and this place. I hoped that meant they'd be okay. We stood and watched them drive down the road until they became no more than tiny specs.

It was just the six of us again.

Oh, and the helicopter pilot, of course.

"Come on," Isaac called to us, taking long strides across the grass in the direction of the helicopter. Jonathan had already gotten behind the controls, and now the big machine was warming up, the rotor blades spinning faster and faster. It was already loud, the roar of the engine increasing. I ducked my head and ran for the chopper. The other guys moved beside me, each mimicking my movements, keeping low and running at a jog.

"How are you all doing?" Jonathan asked, shouting over the roar of the helicopter. "I hear we're heading home."

"That's right," Isaac yelled back as he pulled himself on board. He took one of the seats behind the pilot. "We got enough fuel to make it?"

Jonathan nodded. "Barely. Good thing we refueled when we did."

The idea of stopping once more to refuel would have driven me crazy with frustration. We needed to be back at the base right now, but such a thing was impossible.

I climbed into the second row, with Clay taking the seat on one side of me, and Lorcan the other. Alex moved into the back row, directly behind us, and Kingsley climbed on board and sat next to Isaac.

Jonathan slammed the doors of the helicopter behind us, and then climbed in the front. "Everyone ready?" he called back.

We each nodded, and then proceeded to pull the headphone from the backs of our seats and settle them over our heads. I immediately felt more comfortable without the sound drilling against my eardrums, but I was never going to relax completely. I didn't know what we were going to discover when we got back to base, and my mind kept conjuring up images of what we'd found at the Atlanta location. I was terrified of us finding the same thing.

The roar of the helicopter blades increased, and then we lifted into the air. I held my breath, finding this transition between being on the ground to being airborne the worst part about traveling in one of these things. People might think it was glamorous, but all I felt was uneasy. I'd only been in an airplane a handful of times, but even they seemed more stable than this thing.

But as we reached a cruising altitude, I forced myself to relax a little. We had a few hours until we got back to our base, and I'd be a nervous wreck if I couldn't bring myself to chill out. I took a couple of deep, slow breaths, trying to calm my heartrate.

"You okay?" Clay asked me through the headset.

I looked to him and forced a smile. "I'm working on it."

He returned the closed lipped smile and nodded. "Yeah, I know what you mean."

I always thought of the guys as being tough, and not letting any of this affect them, but I guessed that wasn't the truth. I didn't want any harm coming to anyone at the base, and of course I loved my aunt, but that place had been their home since they were children. They'd grown up with the people there, and had watched the boys there grow and learn. The truth was that however much I felt this thing between me and Hollan was personal, they had far more invested in this than I did.

As we left the base behind us, I leaned over to look out the window. I was frightened that I had gotten things wrong, and the leaving vehicles containing the children would come face to face with Hollan and his men coming in the opposite direction. Though I didn't want that to happen, at least then we'd know the reason Devlin wasn't answering his phone, and Isaac couldn't make contact with the D.C. base, was because of something less innocuous than we were imagining.

With time on our hands, we took the opportunity to figure out what our move would be when we arrived. Isaac used both his phone and laptop to try to contact base again, but only got the same result. It seemed unlikely that the reason no one was answering was because they were busy. Something was preventing them from making contact, and whatever that something was probably wasn't going to be good.

"I suggest we circle the clearing where the base is located before we do anything else. It might be obvious from above what we're about to walk into. Hollan won't have walked there. There will be vehicles around."

"He might have left the vehicles a distance away, and sneaked in through the tree line," Lorcan suggested.

Isaac nodded. "Yeah, that's possible, but we'll be able to do a flyover and see if there's any unusual vehicles around."

"That won't be much good if they've used the tree cover."

Isaac's lips thinned, and I watched his shoulders tense and his eyes narrow. "You got any better suggestions?"

Lorcan shook his head and glanced away. I didn't like seeing them fight, but tensions were high. I knew Isaac only wanted to do the right thing.

"There'll be some kind of disturbance," I offered. "Devlin wouldn't have just let them in."

"How do we know that? Hollan might still have the boys he took from the Atlanta base. What if he threatens to shoot the kids unless he opens up?"

My stomach twisted. I couldn't imagine being in Devlin's position to make that kind of choice. He'd want to protect the boys he had down in the base, while wanting to save the lives of the ones Hollan had. It would be an impossible decision.

"Maybe Devlin will be able to talk to Hollan on a different level? Try to reason with him."

Isaac arched an eyebrow at me. "You think Hollan is a reasonable man, love?"

No, I didn't, and Isaac knew that.

Like Lorcan had done, I glanced away.

The truth was that there was little we could do to prepare for what we might be about to face.

Chapter Thirteen

The time on board the helicopter seemed to pass frustratingly slowly.

But it did pass, and before I thought I could ever be ready, we were approaching our home base. Nerves swirled in my stomach, making me lightheaded, and my heartbeat felt like the flutter of a trapped butterfly's wings against the inside of my ribcage. I alternated squeezing myself tight, my arms compressed against my torso, and stretching out to try to relieve some of the tension.

My hands shook as I checked my gun, making sure it was still fully loaded, even though I had yet to shoot a bullet. I felt sick with fear about what we might find, and prayed my hunch had been wrong. Around me, the men did the same thing, checking their weapons and making sure they had plenty of ammo on hand for reloading. We didn't know what we were going to be dropping in on, and we wanted to be prepared.

"We're approaching the area now, folks," Jonathan said over the headset. "You might want to keep an eye out the window, watch for anything that looks out of place."

I did as he instructed and leaned over Clay to look out at the ground below us. The helicopter started to descend, bringing the green blobs of trees and the gray snakes of roads into focus. There wasn't much out here—it was mainly forest—but I strained my eyes trying to pick out any detail, spot anything that would give us a clue as to what was happening.

The chopper dipped lower again, and through the trees, I spotted the tall, rusted equipment of the abandoned logging site. My breath caught. We were back. Jonathan circled the area, sweeping down over the tops of the trees, so the clearing of the logging site where the entrance to the base was located came into full view. I wanted to grab hold of Clay's hand beside me, but instead I reached to my hip and wrapped my fingers around the handle of my gun. The weapon would provide me with more protection than holding a man's hand right now, however much I wanted to.

We were all doing the same thing, peering out the side windows of the chopper, trying to see if there was anything different we should be aware of, but, from as high up as we were, it was impossible to tell.

"Can you take her lower, Jonathan?" Isaac asked over the headset.

"Sure."

The helicopter banked sharply to the right and started coming back around. We were going to circle back over the area. He brought the chopper lower, so it almost brushed the tops of the trees. The downward draft the huge machine created caused the branches of the trees to fan outward, leaves and twigs flying into the air, only to be whipped away by the rotor blades.

I had no doubt that if Hollan was somewhere around, he'd certainly have noticed our arrival.

"There's nothing," Isaac said through the headset. "Maybe we should set her down."

Jonathan called back, "Can do, boss."

He brought the aircraft back around, aiming to land in the clearing.

Suddenly, there was a loud crack, and Jonathan jerked to one side, a spatter of red droplets spraying onto the glass. The helicopter banked heavily to the left, throwing us all in that direction, and a scream escaped my throat. Confusion and panic filled me. Amid the chaos of the helicopter lurching out of control, I tried to piece together what had happened. Not only was the helicopter starting to turn in a spin, there was a small hole through the pilot's window. Because of the noise of the engine and the wop-wop of the blades, it had been hard to hear, but someone had shot us from the ground.

"Oh, shit!"

In front of me, Isaac's fingers went to his belt, and he fumbled with the buckle. The world had gone mad around us, the whirring of the blades suddenly a pitch higher, or perhaps it was the engine, I wasn't sure.

The ground was coming up too fast.

Then Isaac was out of his seat and lurching forward.

"Isaac, no!"

If we were going to crash, I didn't want him to not be strapped in.

He stepped and fell, bouncing off the side of one of the seats. I realized what he was doing, trying to reach the pilot. Jonathan had fallen across the level which controlled the helicopter's movement, which was why the helicopter had gone into a spin. Isaac managed to regain his balance and leaned over the seat, hauling the pilot up. I'd seen the impact of the bullet, the way the other side of his head had exploded, leaving tiny pieces of skull and brain matter across the seat. At no point did I hold any hope that he might have survived.

Kingsley must have understood what Isaac was doing, as he unclipped himself as well and followed his movements. The aircraft continued to spin, leaving me sickeningly dizzy. I'd braced myself for impact, expecting the blades to strike the ground or the surrounding trees at any moment, and the helicopter bursting into a huge fireball with us in it. I didn't want it to end this way. Not now. Not like this. Fingers reached for mine, and I looked down to see Clay holding my hand tight. I could see the fear in his eyes, but with it he also fixed me in his gaze. *Look at me. Focus on me. Don't think about what might be about to happen.*

But the motion of the aircraft slowed, and I risked looking away to see Isaac and Kingsley at the front. Kingsley had hold of the body of the pilot, pulling him away from the controls, while Isaac leaned forward, pulling on the lever, I assumed, and trying to stabilize the helicopter.

I had no idea if Isaac knew how to fly this thing. It wasn't something he'd ever mentioned before. The helicopter had stopped its furious spin which had sent the world into a blur around us, but it still felt far from under control. The machine dipped and then rose, lurching to one side, and then the other, like a giant beast that had been shot with a sedative dart and no longer had control of itself.

"We're going down!" Isaac yelled. "Brace yourselves."

I'd been bracing myself since the moment I understood what was happening. The shriek of the helicopter was too much. The headphones had been ripped from my head from all the movement, but I couldn't have pinpointed the moment when it had happened. Then arms wrapped around me from behind, and Clay leaned across the front of me, as though hoping to pin me in my seat. Alex held my other shoulder, perhaps knowing it wouldn't do much good, but trying to offer me some comfort. And it did. They'd surrounded me with their bodies. Trying to protect me, even though we had no idea what might happen next. Hell, yes, we did. We were going to crash.

Oh God, oh God, oh God, oh God.

Panic and terror flitted through my mind, every muscle bunched. I didn't want to think of Isaac and Kingsley at the front, with no seatbelts on. Or who'd taken the shot at the helicopter and killed the pilot. This had all happened so fast, the time passing by both terrifyingly fast, and also impossibly slowly, as though my brain had slowed every moment, so I would be aware of the final minutes of my life in pure, three-dimensional detail.

The helicopter hit the ground, but instead of the nosedive I was expecting, the landing skids somehow struck the forest floor first. The chopper bounced and lifted back into the air, before coming down again. The blades still spun, though I thought they might be slowing. We were somehow still moving forward, and I risked glancing up to see the tree trunks of the forest growing larger through the front windshield. The engine suddenly died around us, and we were left with only the whirring of the blades above our heads as their momentum slowed. Isaac must have somehow killed the power.

There was an impossible silence before we struck the line of trees. And then we were thrown forward, combined with a horrific crunch, metal screeching on metal, glass shattering. My head whipped forward and snapped back, slamming the back of my skull into the seat behind.

And then everything fell still.

Chapter Fourteen

The acrid stench of spilled diesel filled my nostrils and made my eyes water. Around my head, pieces of metal creaked and clicked, and another shard of glass fell from one of the windows and shattered with a crash, followed by a tinkle. My seatbelt had held, though it had crushed the air out of my lungs, and I knew I would be sporting some serious bruising across my chest. But I'd somehow survived.

My attention turned to the others. Were they all right?

Beside me, Clay shifted, sitting upright. "You okay, sugar?" His voice was a croak.

"Yeah, I think so." I looked around, frantic. *Isaac, Kingsley!* "What about the others?"

On my left, Lorcan groaned. "Fuck. Someone shot the pilot from the ground." He sat up straighter then reached to unclip his seatbelt. "They'll be coming here next."

Oh, my God. I knew what that meant. We needed to move and fast. We were sitting ducks by staying here.

I twisted slightly in my seat, the movement causing pain to lance up through my chest. "You okay, Alex?"

Behind me, Alex coughed and budged in his seat. "Yeah, I'm okay."

Movement came from the front, someone moaning. We'd hit the trees with both Isaac and Kingsley right at the front of the chopper, and neither of them had been strapped in. Kingsley's big body was slumped across the back of the passenger seat. Isaac wasn't even in view. Had he been thrown from the helicopter? Frantic, I reached to my belt buckle, my fingers feeling numb and fat. Terror clutched at my chest, and I feared the worst. Where was Isaac? I wanted to cry, but I wasn't going to let myself. I didn't have the luxury of tears right now.

I needed to get to them, to make sure they were all right. At the front of the helicopter, with no seatbelts on, there was no way they could have gone uninjured when we hit the trees.

"How far away have we come down?" Clay asked.

I shook my head. "I have no idea." Everything had been so disorienting when we'd lost control of the helicopter. I thought we'd come down somewhere in the clearing, but I had no idea where.

Lorcan worked to free himself from the restraints of the belt, too. "It's not going to take the shooters long to get here."

Shit. We were being stalked on the ground by whoever had killed Jonathan. I couldn't think about the pilot being dead. He'd seemed like a decent guy, but I'd barely spoken to him. He might have had a family we didn't even know about, people who would need to be informed of his death.

My belt popped, and as I staggered on trembling legs toward the front of the helicopter, I reached to the holster at my waist and pulled my gun free. Movement came beside me, and I looked to find Alex right there.

"Cover us," he called back to Lorcan and Clay. "We need to check on the others."

I knew what that meant. Lorcan and Clay were going to need to cover us from the men who were most likely now approaching the helicopter from the outside. They'd shoot us as soon as they reached us, and if Alex and I were focusing on Kingsley and Isaac, we wouldn't be able to protect ourselves.

As Alex and I climbed over the seats to get to the front of the helicopter, Lorcan reached over and managed to wrench open the side door. We hit the trees from the front on, which meant, other than some buckling, the doors were still intact.

I managed to peer over the seat. Isaac was on the floor of the helicopter, folded into a position that didn't look natural at all. "Oh, God."

Scrambling over the back of the seat, I planted both my feet on the pilot's seat. Jonathan's body had slumped to one side when he'd been shot, and then thrown farther when we'd crashed. I tried not to look at the blood spatters, or the way the poor man appeared to be missing a chunk of his skull. I needed to focus on those of us who were still alive. Isaac had been thrown directly over the back of his seat and into the small space where the control panel was located. I kneeled and reached down to Isaac. Was he still breathing?

I folded his arms away from his face so I could get a better look. His hands and forearms were cut up from the glass. Blood soaked into the white of his shirt, and the gray sleeves of his suit jacket. A bloom of watercolor dripped onto canvas.

His eyes were shut, his lips slightly parted. More blood matted the light brown of his hairline, creating a rusty halo. I placed my fingers beneath his nose, desperately trying to figure out if I could feel the heat of his breath. Could I detect the faintest warming of my skin, or was I imagining things?

"How is he?" Alex called to me.

"I'm... I'm not sure."

Then his arm jerked, and his eyes flickered open. "Oh, thank God." I twisted to Alex. "He's alive."

"So is Kingsley. Come on, buddy. Time to wake up now." We wouldn't be able to carry Kingsley out of here. Not with armed men hunting us down. He was too big, and would mean we wouldn't be able to move fast enough. I was suddenly relieved we'd handed George over to Andrea when we'd had the chance. I couldn't imagine being in this situation with a kid. It was terrifying enough.

"I can see movement in the distance!" Lorcan yelled from where he was positioned beside the now open doorway. Clay had taken up position on the opposite side of the helicopter, so we were covered from both directions. "They're coming."

It wasn't much, but at least we had the shell of the aircraft to take shelter in. I turned my attention back to our leader.

"Isaac, are you okay?"

He groaned and winced, but managed to nod, He grappled out, trying to right himself. I took his hand to try to pull him upright. He winced again, and I noticed the hand I was holding had a gash in the palm. His skin was slippery and hot against mine. But he seemed to be becoming more and more aware with every second that passed.

His gaze, at first unfocused, finally settled on my face. "We landed?"

I held back a small, crazed laugh. "We're on the ground, if that counts?"

A muscle beside his right eye twitched. "Yeah, I guess it'll have to."

I helped to pull him up, so his feet were on the floor instead of his backside. The space was small, and he was hurt, but we managed it.

I ran my hands down his body in a purely practical way, checking him over and making sure he didn't have any huge pieces of glass speared into his body that shock hadn't yet let him recognize. But, apart from all the cuts from the glass, and the wound in his scalp, he appeared to be unharmed.

"I think he's okay," I called back to Alex.

"I'll be even better if you keep doing that to me, love." One side of his lips quirked in a smile, and I had to hold myself back from smacking him. In the chaos of the crash, he seemed to have forgotten what a dangerous situation we were in. His gaze was still dreamy, as though he'd had a little too much to drink.

"How's Kingsley?" I asked Alex, ignoring Isaac's comment. He didn't know what he was saying.

"Cut up," Alex replied, "but he's coming around. Slowly."

Clay shouted from his position at the back of the helicopter. "They're almost here. Prepare yourselves."

I leaned to one side, looking out the pilot's window. "Where? I can't see them."

"Right there!" Clay replied. "Between the trees. They're using them as cover."

"Sons of bitches," Lorcan swore.

"Hollan's men?" I wanted to confirm.

Clay nodded. "Who else?"

Our proximity to the base meant only one thing. I'd been right when I'd suspected Hollan had doubled back and come here. What had he done with everyone below ground? Were they all dead? Devlin, the boys, my aunt? It was an unthinkable but very real possibility.

"Come on, Kingsley," Alex said, giving the big guy a shake. "You got to wake up, man. We need to get out of here!"

"Can we drag him?" I suggested.

"We can try, but it'll slow us down and make us an easy target."

I remembered the stop we'd made at the hangar, and the snacks we'd bought. Frantic, I scanned the floor of the helicopter, trying to spot something. There, that was what I wanted! A bottle of water. It might not be the most sophisticated method of bringing someone around, but we were desperate. I snatched up the bottle and unscrewed the cap, and then tipped the cool water over Kingsley's head.

He sprang forward, gasping.

I felt guilty for bringing him around in such a way, but at least he was awake. Even more importantly, he was alive.

"Fuck." He wiped his hand over his face, and then winced. "What happened?"

"We can't go over it now. Can you walk?"

He looked around, confused. "The chopper ... it was going down."

"Seriously, Kingsley," I said. We didn't have time to explain what had happened. "You need to move or we're all going to end up dead. Can you walk?"

He nodded. "Yeah, I think so." He hauled his massive frame upright in the confined space, and then caught sight of Jonathan and the crushed fuselage of the helicopter. His eyes widened at the sight, but thankfully he didn't ask any more questions.

Lorcan leaned out the door and fired a couple of shots. The bangs were impossibly loud, and I flinched with each crack, my ears already ringing from the noise of the helicopter crash.

"Go!" he yelled. "Into the tree line. I'll cover you."

"No, there's too many of them." And there were. I risked taking a peek to see numerous men in the same black protective gear we'd watched on the video approaching with their weapons aimed.

My hand went to my hip, checking my gun was still there. It was. "I'll help cover, too. Alex and Clay, help Isaac and Kingsley get to the tree line."

Lorcan glanced back at me. "No, Darcy. You go."

"I'm not strong enough to help the men, but I know how to shoot."

Lorcan threw me a look, and then, perhaps seeing the determination on my face, gave me a short nod. I took the opposite side, stepping into Clay's place as Clay moved back to help Alex move Kingsley. Using the interior of the helicopter as cover, we leaned out the side to take shots at the approaching men.

"Aim for the neck, arms, or legs," Lorcan yelled to me between shots. "They won't be protected by bulletproof gear on those areas."

I refocused and did what he instructed. I lined my sight on one man as he jogged forward, his weapon aimed at the fallen chopper. I pulled the trigger. The gun recoiled, bucking in my hands, and the man jerked to the side, as though someone had shoulder barged him. A volley of gunfire returned, punching holes in the metal door of the helicopter. *Thwack, thwack, thwack.* I cowered, half-expecting a bullet to strike me at any moment.

Gunfire came from closer to the tree line, and I realized the guys had made it. They were able to cover us now.

"Come on," Lorcan said, reaching out to grab my hand. I allowed him to pull me out of the chopper, and just as Clay and Alex fired at the approaching men, we took the opportunity to run. My whole body hurt from the crash, but I ignored the pain, knowing we needed to get to relative safety. Even breathing hurt my lungs from where the straps had tightened across my chest, bruising my ribs. None of that mattered now, though. We were alive, and I wanted it to stay that way.

We scrambled away. I expected for a bullet to punch me in the back, but we reached where the others were hiding and threw ourselves behind the thick tree trunks to take shelter. Now I could see the helicopter properly, my blood curdled in my veins. We'd been so incredibly lucky to survive that. Then I remembered not all of us had.

Chapter Fifteen

Hollan's men kept coming, closing the distance between us. Now I had a better view, I counted them. There were four men left now, with two injured, having taken bullets from me and Lorcan.

Kingsley had slumped down behind one of the tree trunks, but he held his gun and leaned out to fire at the approaching men.

"Can you see Hollan anywhere?" Isaac yelled.

Lorcan frowned. "No, but it's hard to tell with them wearing headgear."

"Shit."

I shook my head. "He won't be there. He always gets others to do his dirty work."

"Then we're going to need to find out where he is." Lorcan peered back around the side of the trunk, and then darted away, to the left, using each of the trees as cover. I only caught flashes of his black leather jacket as he moved between them.

"What's he doing?" I hissed.

Isaac shook his head, his expression as baffled as my own. "I'm not sure."

There was no time to talk about things. The men were closing in on us. But they were exposed, where we had cover. More smart shots from the guys took another couple of men down. I tried to spot Lorcan, trying to see where he'd gone.

Suddenly, he stepped out into the open, behind where the remaining two men still moved forward. My breath caught in my lungs, my whole body freezing as I stared in shocked horror at him, wondering what the hell he was playing at. He crept forward, moving quickly and almost silently up behind one of the remaining two. In what appeared to be two actions at once, he pointed his gun and fired a bullet into one of the men's leg, and wrapped his arm around the second man's throat. He lifted his foot and kicked the gun out of the shot soldier's hand. The man he had by the throat fought back, firing a shot that made me sick to my stomach, but that missed Lorcan, thank God. Lorcan wrestled the gun from him, and then yanked off the man's helmet. The headgear fell to the ground, rolling in the dirt.

The man with the leg wound reached for the gun he'd dropped, but Clay was there before he could reach it. I hadn't even noticed Clay leave our side. Clay kicked the weapon away, and it skidded some distance in the dirt before coming to a standstill, well out of reach.

Isaac marched out. I could see he was overcompensating for the injuries he had suffered in the crash, but he didn't want to show any weakness. He aimed his gun at the man on the ground, while Lorcan still had hold of the other one, the muzzle of his gun now jammed into the side of the man's head.

"Where the fuck is Hollan?" Isaac demanded. "What's he done to the base? Is he down there?"

The soldier on the ground clutched his bleeding leg. "I don't know."

Isaac took a step closer. "You don't want to die for that son of a bitch, trust me."

Lorcan jammed the muzzle harder against the other man's head, his upper lip curling in a snarl. I recognized this side of Lorcan—the cold, merciless side. It frightened me a little, but he got the job done.

The man on the ground lifted one hand from his gunshot wound to wave it in the air in self-defense. "Okay, okay. He's down there. He jammed the communication system, and overrode the electronics so he could get in."

"So he's down there now?" Isaac confirmed.

The man nodded.

"How many men does he have with him?"

"The same as he left up here," the soldier blurted. "Six."

"And where are the boys he took from Atlanta?"

Confusion crossed the man's pale face. "I don't know. Not here."

Isaac frowned. "What do you mean, not here?"

"He said it was a separate part of the mission, and left with them and a couple of the guys. I don't know where they went, or why."

My stomach sank. The boys weren't here. Fuck. Where the hell had he taken them, and why? I was worried for them, but that concern only entangled with my fears for the people currently underground with Hollan and his men. Were they still alive? Had they fought back? Had my aunt managed to leave before they'd arrived?

"We have to get down there," I said.

Clay pressed his lips together and glanced between us. "He'll already know we're here."

Isaac shrugged. "There's nothing we can do about that."

Kingsley emerged from behind the trees to join us, limping and holding his side. Alex was with him, too, helping him along.

This all felt futile. How were we going to help the people in the base? Where had the boys been taken?

I looked between the men, my eyes wide. "We have to go down there."

Lorcan's jaw was rigid as he replied. "Hollan's men are going to shoot us the minute we step out of the elevator."

"Then we'll just have to shoot faster," Isaac said.

Clay shook his head. "This is insane."

Lorcan jerked his chin at the two men we'd taken down. "We use them as protection. Hold them in front of us as we're going down, and the moment those doors open, we start firing."

The man with the gunshot wound whimpered in pain. I'd almost have felt sorry for him if he hadn't been shooting at us ten minutes earlier.

"We won't all fit inside the elevator," I pointed out.

"I'll go down," Lorcan continued. "I'll take Isaac and Clay."

I bit my lower lip. "I don't like this."

He stared back at me. "We don't have any choice."

Lorcan was right. There was no way we were going to walk away from this. My aunt was down there, together with innocent children. There was no scenario where we'd abandon them and leave Hollan to do whatever he wanted.

I thought of something. "How are we going to get the elevator to come up? We can't call it from the outside."

"I've never needed to look for it," Isaac said, "but there's supposed to be a failsafe somewhere close by that can be used in case of an emergency or power cut."

"I'd say this probably qualifies as an emergency," I pointed out. "Isn't there another way in? An emergency escape route?"

He nodded. "Yes, there is. But it can only be opened from the inside. So unless we can get someone to open it for us, we're going to have to find the failsafe for the elevator."

Still keeping our weapons trained on the two men, we made our way over to the hatch for the elevator shaft.

Clay and Lorcan remained standing guard over the two men, while Alex, Isaac, and I started to hunt. Kingsley joined in as well, but he was moving slowly, and I could read the pain etched in his face.

"What are we looking for, Isaac?" Alex called out.

"Not sure. A lever or push button of some kind."

We continued to search, swiping our hands through the dirt and tufts of grass.

"Got it," Alex yelled, and he lifted his hand and brought it down on the switch.

The whirr of the elevator started from deep beneath the ground, and we all stepped back.

"Get ready," Isaac warned. "There might be people inside."

By people, I knew he meant Hollan's men.

Lorcan shrugged but raised his gun, aiming it at the elevator shaft. "That's only if they know we're here. If Hollan cut the communication, could that mean he did the same for the security cameras?"

Clay lifted his eyebrows and pushed his hand through his hair, but like Lorcan, he kept his gun trained on where the elevator would appear. "That would have been a pretty dumb move."

"But if he only had the choice of taking it all out, or taking none of it out, I guess he's going to have gone with all of it."

I hoped he was right. Was there a chance Hollan didn't know we were here?

Isaac perhaps knew what I was thinking. "Don't get complacent. Go in there assuming Hollan knows everything."

I nodded.

The elevator rose behind him, and he hauled the man he had hold of, twisting his body so the other man was directly in front of him. Maybe he would have fought more, but he had a gun pressed to his head, and he'd already seen his friend shot in the leg, and most of the others killed. Perhaps he hoped being taken down to Hollan would be his best chance.

Everyone braced themselves as the doors slid open, expecting men to start shooting at us from inside the car, but they revealed only empty space. There was no time to relax, however.

Isaac turned and looked at me, and then his gaze flicked to Kingsley. "You should stay here, take care of Kingsley."

I shook my head, my heart flipping. "No, I know what you're doing. I'm coming down with you."

"This is dangerous. You might end up hurt, or dead."

"So? So might you, or Lorcan, or Clay. You can't make me stay behind, not after everything. I need to see this through. I understand you're trying to protect me, not just from Hollan, but from what we might find when we get down there. But I'm one of you now, and you can't protect me just because I'm a girl."

"It's not because you're a girl, Darcy. It's because we love you, and the thought of anything happening to you is worse than the idea of us dying ourselves."

I put my hands on my hips. "Well, I feel the same way about you, but you don't see me telling you to stay behind."

Kingsley shook his head, too. "We're all coming. You need as many people on your side as you can get."

Isaac glared at him, and Kingsley glanced over at me, realization dawning across his face.

"We'll come back for you," Isaac said.

Isaac shoved the man forward, and Lorcan moved with the one who'd been shot in the leg, using him as a human shield. The man whimpered and limped, so Lorcan basically had to drag him. Lorcan wasn't a big man, but he was fiercely strong, every inch of his body covered in muscle. With his fist bunched in the man's jacket, he dragged him into the elevator.

My heart was in my throat. I didn't want to watch them vanish out of view, knowing they could be killed seconds later, as soon as the doors opened on the next level.

"We'll keep going down," Isaac said, as though reading my thoughts. "They won't expect us to head right to the bottom. It should take them by surprise."

"We're following," I called. "Send the elevator back up."

Isaac didn't reply, his face stern as the doors slid shut, blocking them from view. Hot tears burned the back of my throat.

"We're going after them," I said, looking to Kingsley and Alex. "I don't care what Isaac said."

Kingsley nodded. "Yeah, we're going after them."

I braced myself, wondering if we'd be able to hear gunfire from below, but everything was silent.

Miraculously, within a couple of minutes, the elevator reappeared.

"Move to one side," Kingsley said, his voice rough.

Using his body, he barged me out of direct view of the front of the elevator. Despite his injuries, with his limp and the way he clutched his ribs, he positioned his body in front of mine and aimed his gun toward the elevator to protect me. I wanted to feel like I could protect myself, but I still found my heart swelling with love for the way he was taking care of me.

But the doors slid open, and once again, the space was empty.

I pushed past Kingsley to get to the car. My gaze took in every detail, trying to spot signs of bullet holes, splatters of blood, empty shell casings. I even inhaled, in case I picked up on the hint of gunpowder or blood on the air. There was a smear of red on the floor, but I figured that could easily have come from the man with the bullet wound in his leg.

Kingsley and Alex joined me.

"What level?" My finger hovered above the buttons. Did we go to the bottom level, and hope to join the others, or mix things up a little?

Alex looked at me. "If someone has noticed the elevator moving, they might have chased it down to the bottom level. If we stop sooner, we might catch them off guard."

I sucked in a breath. "Good point."

I hesitated, not knowing what to do.

Kingsley leaned in and hit the button for the control floor. "If he's there, let's take the son of a bitch head on."

We shared a glance, nodding in agreement, and then both men stepped in front of me, shielding me from whatever was coming next.

Chapter Sixteen

The doors slid shut, encasing us inside the metal box, and then we were moving down.

Tension seemed to radiate from the walls, as though they knew what was about to happen. I held my breath, sensing the men in front of me do the same.

The elevator jolted to a halt. Right before the doors opened, we all stepped to the sides—Kingsley and I to the left, and Alex to the right—so that if anyone was in front of us, all they'd see as the doors opened was an empty space.

The men didn't stay in that position for long. The doors began to open, and, as soon as the gap was big enough, they burst into action. Leaning out only far enough to shoot, they fired a couple of shots. I heard a cry, and then a thud as some hit the floor.

A different person, I assumed, fired in return, and Kingsley darted back again. Opposite us, Alex leaned out and squeezed off a couple more shots. We received more return fire, and the bullets lodged into the metal of the back of the elevator car. I froze and held my breath, but everything had stopped, the silence deafening.

Kingsley and Alex both leaned out again. Apparently not seeing anything immediately threatening, they both stepped out, Alex jerking his head toward the exit to tell me to do the same. I quickly took in the scene before us. Two men, who I assumed were the people the guys had just shot, were on the ground in front of us. A little farther away, another man lay dead, but this one I recognized as being one of our own.

But something other than the bodies caught my eye.

Devlin was in a chair, his hands cuffed behind his back, and something shoved in his mouth to stop him from talking. His eyes widened at the sight of us, and he started to struggle. Considering the other man had been killed, I wondered why Devlin had been taken hostage rather than executed.

"It's okay," Alex said, rushing toward him. "We're getting you out of here."

"Where's Hollan?" I demanded, though I knew he couldn't talk yet. "Did you see the others? Isaac, Lorcan, and Clay? What about my aunt? Is she still alive?" The sight of the other bodies filled me with dread. They'd been executed. Had the same fate met my aunt and the other boys?

Devlin still couldn't speak. There was no point in me firing questions at him until we had the cloth out of his mouth.

Alex reached him first, and yanked it out. Devlin sucked in a breath and started to cough.

"Where's everyone else?" Alex asked. "Where's Hollan?"

"I don't know." Devlin started to cough again, but managed to control himself enough to speak. "He went to the lower levels. He left those men you shot to guard me and took the others with him. He noticed the elevator working and figured he hadn't given anyone instruction to move around."

Kingsley looked to the surveillance screens. "So he wasn't watching us on the cameras?"

For the first time, I noticed they were all blank.

Devlin shook his head. "No. He did something to the communication systems down here and took out our cameras at the same time."

I remembered one of the guys outside saying that Hollan had shut down the communications systems. That must have included surveillance and explained why the screens were all blank. He'd handicapped Devlin and the others down here by not giving them a way to communicate with the outside world, but he'd also handicapped himself by not being able to see what was happening outside. I was sure someone had called down to him when they'd spotted the helicopter coming in, and probably had notified him when we'd gone down, too. But otherwise I didn't know how much Hollan had known about what had gone on aboveground.

Or had he predicted what we were going to do, and planned for this all along? Were we being herded into a trap, as easily as sheep chased by a dog?

Still, my thoughts were with Isaac and the others, and with Aunt Sarah and the other boys.

Alex moved forward to where Devlin's hands were cuffed to the chair. "Shit. I don't suppose he left a key anywhere?"

Devlin shook his head. "Can't you pick it?"

"I can try, but I don't know how long it's going to take. Those cuffs are top of the range."

I chewed my lip, hopping from foot to foot. I was desperate to find my aunt and the boys. "The others need us."

"Just go," said Devlin. "I'll be fine. Get Hollan and put a god-damned bullet in the back of his head. I'm sick to death of the son of a bitch."

I nodded in agreement. "That makes two of us."

Meanwhile, Hollan could be anywhere in the building.

I remembered the plan my aunt had been putting into place before we'd left. "Is Sarah safe?" I asked Devlin. "Is she with the boys?"

He shook his head. "I'm sorry. I don't know."

I looked to Kingsley and Alex. "I need to find them."

"We'll come with you," Alex replied.

"No, you need to find Hollan."

Kingsley fixed me with his dark gaze. "There's no way in hell we're letting you go alone, Darcy."

"This is a big place. I know it better than Hollan. I can sneak around. Besides, you're still hurt, Kingsley. I can see you're trying to hide it, but you're big and you're limping. You'll get us noticed. I can be quick, and will get my aunt and the boys out of here."

I could see Kingsley was starting to waver. He didn't want to let me go, and I understood that, but he also knew I was talking sense.

"Besides, we can't unlock Devlin. Who's going to protect him when Hollan comes back? 'Cause you know he *will* come back."

It was a low blow. I'd known Kingsley's loyalties were torn between me and his boss.

"Fine," he relented. "I'll stay here with Devlin, but you're taking Alex with you."

I looked to Alex, and he nodded.

"Okay." I had to admit I felt safer with Alex by my side, even if it did mean leaving Kingsley hurt and Devlin still handcuffed. But even an injured Kingsley was still a force to be reckoned with.

Alex checked the magazine in his gun, making sure he had enough bullets. "We just have to hope Isaac and the others were able to locate Hollan. You never know, they might have even dealt with him already."

I pulled a face. "As much as I want to believe you, Alex, my gut tells me otherwise."

"Yeah. Me, too."

The levels were pretty well insulated for sound, but we hadn't heard any telltale gunfire. Did Hollan even know we were in the building? Had Isaac found him yet?

We made sure Kingsley had enough weapons and bullets to protect himself and Devlin.

I looked down to see Alex's hand on my arm. "Come on," he said, "we'll take the stairs."

I'd never needed to take this route before. Everyone always used the elevators to get around, but there was an emergency staircase, just in case the power went down and the generators didn't kick in.

I paused, and then spun back to Kingsley, wrapping my arms around his neck and squeezing him tight. He sucked a breath in over his teeth, and I leaned back so I could see into his face. "Sorry," I said, realizing I'd hurt him.

He gave me a gentle smile. "You're fine."

I placed my hand against his cheek, his skin velvety soft beneath the start of dark stubble. "Be careful, okay."

He nodded. "You, too."

Leaning in, I kissed him quickly, not caring that Devlin was there. The rules had all changed now, and I knew how fast things could go wrong. If this was the last time I ever got to see him, I wanted to be able to remember I'd at least kissed him goodbye. I lingered, my fingers on his skin, not wanting to leave him.

"We have to go," Alex called.

I had to think of those boys and my aunt.

I nodded and forced myself away, following Alex to a door at the back of the control room, on the opposite side to the elevator. It had a bar across the middle, which Alex depressed, allowing the door to swing open. Darkness lay beyond, but the moment Alex stepped through, a light flickered on. It must have been controlled by a motion sensor.

Following Alex's long, lean form, I hurried down the stairs. I held my gun at my side, my fingers tight around the grip. I didn't know if Hollan's men knew about this access route, but I was prepared for them anyway.

"Where's your aunt supposed to be hiding with the boys?" Alex called back to me, his voice low.

"In the gun range, right at the back. That's what we'd agreed on, anyway, but there's no saying they'll still be there. Hollan or his men might have found them, or they thought they were going to be found, and so they moved themselves."

"Well, we'll find out soon enough."

We reached the bottom of the stairwell, and pushed out onto the floor where the gun range was located. It was still too quiet, and the silence unnerved me. Where was Hollan? Where were Isaac, Clay, and Lorcan? Had something happened to them? I needed to focus on my aunt and the boys, but I couldn't stop my mind wandering.

We pushed out of the doors, side by side, checking to make sure the corridor was empty. There was no sign of anyone. We sneaked out, both of us moving at a run now, staying on tiptoes to try to reduce the noise. My heart thrummed in my chest, filled with the terrible anticipation that all we'd find in the gun range were the bodies of my aunt and the children.

At the end of the corridor, we reached the door for the gun range. The light wasn't on to say it was occupied, but then I figured they wouldn't exactly have wanted to advertise their presence. Because the gun range was soundproofed, it was impossible for us to hear if there was any movement happening inside.

I felt physically sick as I tried the door, terrified of what I might find.

It was locked.

Of course it was locked. I didn't know why I'd considered for a single minute that Sarah wouldn't have locked the door behind her. As soon as she heard the base being attacked, she would have brought the boys down here and locked them in to keep them safe. That was the main thing to focus on. If they were inside this room, it meant they were okay.

"Aunt Sarah?" I hissed against the door. I tried to remember if the door itself was soundproofed. I thought it might have been, but I couldn't remember for sure.

I didn't want to raise my voice, knowing it might be heard by the wrong people. But, assuming she was here, she needed to know I was here and that we were going to get them out.

"It's me, Aunt Sarah. Are you there?" I increased my hiss to a louder call.

"It's soundproofed," Alex said. "She's not going to hear you." He nudged me to one side. "Let's try this instead."

He reached to the left of the door and hit the button that would cause a light to flash above the inside of the door, and alert whoever was inside to there being someone who needed to get in. Problem was, Sarah had no way of knowing it was us. We could just have easily have been Hollan and his men.

I looked up to Alex, my eyes wide. "What if she won't open the door? She has no way of knowing it's us."

He stared back at me, his blue gaze meeting mine. "I'm not sure."

We couldn't leave here without them. They'd need to come out at some point. But what if something terrible happened and this place came down around their heads. They'd be trapped.

I pushed Alex's hand out of the way and tried the buzzer myself. I willed Sarah to understand that it was us here, and not Hollan, trying to push the essence of myself out to her. I knew it was crazy, willing her to do something—it wasn't as though we had some kind of psychic connection—but I didn't know what else to do.

My mind flitted through options.

"Wait. If I press this buzzer, the light inside flashes on, right?"

Alex nodded. "Right."

"So maybe we can use that to get a message to her."

He looked at me as though I was crazy. "What kind of message?"

"One she knows I'd understand."

I took a breath, and then hit the button three times in quick succession. Then I waited and repeated the process, this time holding the button down for longer each time I pressed it. Then I paused again and hit it three times quickly.

Alex stared at me. "Morse code. You're doing SOS."

I nodded, and repeated what I'd done. I prayed this would work. *Come on, Aunt Sarah. Come on. See what I'm doing here.* I kept hitting the button, repeating the pattern over and over.

To my surprise, the door buzzed open.

I flashed Alex a smile of relief and happiness that it had worked. I moved to take a step inside, but he put out his arm to stop me. "Let me go first. We still don't know for sure that she's the person inside."

I wanted to tell him it was fine, but he was right. I couldn't let my sudden burst of enthusiasm make me reckless.

We stepped through the door and into the space beyond. My eyes adjusted to the dim light. Only the security lights were on around the walls. The space was divided by partitions, and right at the back were the hangings of the silhouettes of people used for targets.

At first I couldn't see anyone, but then the familiar shape of my aunt stepped out from behind one of the partitions. In her hands was a large gun, and it was aimed directly at us, but then she must have realized who we were as she lowered the weapon, and her shoulders visibly dropped.

"Oh, thank God, Darcy. You're safe."

I lowered my own gun and ran to my aunt. We scooped each other up in a hug.

"I was so worried you'd all—" I couldn't say the words. "Where are the boys?" I asked instead.

Something moved behind the targets at the back, and, in the dim light, I spotted a number of pairs of feet. The boys started to appear from behind the target, little heads popping up like cautious rabbits from a burrow.

I exhaled a sigh of relief. They were all here.

I turned my attention back to my aunt. I might have found them, but we were still far from being safe. "Have you seen Hollan?"

She shook her head. "No. We heard shooting and came straight down here, like we'd planned. We've been hiding here, wondering what to do. I didn't want to bring them out, just in case ..."

"You did the right thing. We need to get you all out of here."

"We can fight," one of the older boys said.

Alex stepped in. "We just need to get you somewhere safe. Isaac and the rest of the team are handling everything. You getting involved will only make things more complicated."

The boy seemed to accept what Alex had said. I figured they were all still too frightened to start arguing. They might be being trained for this kind of thing, but they were still years away from being ready. Besides, they were children, and most of them had experienced loss in their lives. Death wasn't an abstract thing they believed would never affect them. They'd already been through enough to know it could strike at any moment, and, when it did, the effects were permanent.

"Come on, let's get out of here. We'll use the stairs. It'll be safer than using the elevators." I hoped I was right. The elevators might be being covered by Hollan's men, but there was no doubt that they would be infinitely faster. I wondered why we still hadn't seen the bastard.

Had he retreated? Had he lost too many men and decided it was time to cut his losses, or had Isaac and the others already killed him? But, if that was the truth, where was Isaac now?

We ushered the boys toward the front of the shooting range. There were twice as many children here as there had been at the other bases, all ranging in age from about seven to twelve. Alex led the way, and I stayed next to my aunt. She looked understandably pale, the skin across her already high cheekbones taut, her mouth thin with worry. I wanted nothing more in that moment than for her to be able to go home, to continue with her life, work hard at her business, and never have to deal with any of this shit again.

"Let's move," Alex hissed back at us, and he pushed the door open with his shoulder. The boys were crowded behind him, and I prayed we wouldn't come face to face with anyone. If a shooting match started, someone was bound to get caught in the crossfire.

We ushered them along the corridor, toward the door to the stairwell.

The heavy *thump-thump-thump* of several feet pounding toward us made Alex lift his hand, telling us all to stop. Leaving my aunt at the back, I slipped past the boys, my gun raised, ready to start shooting. My mouth ran dry, my hands shaking, so I tightened them around my weapon. I pressed my back to the wall, my aunt and the boys behind me doing the same thing.

Alex leaned out, ready to put a bullet in whoever was coming.

Chapter Seventeen

I was frozen against the wall, my heart pounding.

"Hold your fire," Alex called out to me. "It's Isaac and the others."

I slumped with relief. "Oh, thank God."

We rounded the corner together, and I couldn't help but smile as I saw Isaac, Clay and Lorcan walking toward us. They all looked to be uninjured, other than what we'd suffered in the crash. I held myself back from running up to each of them, and hugging and kissing them in turn. Instead, we exchanged smiles of relief, and I could tell simply from the looks in their eyes that they were pleased to see us, too.

A couple of the younger boys ran up to Isaac and Clay, hugging them around their waists. The men looked to Sarah, too, nodding their welcome.

"Thank you for keeping the boys safe," Isaac said to my aunt.

She gave a tight smile. "It was the least I could do."

I noticed they didn't have the other two men with them. "What did you do with the hostages?"

Clay pushed his hand through his hair. "Tied them up in the kitchen and left them there. We hadn't seen any sign of Hollan, and they were slowing us down."

"And the guy with the bullet wound in his leg was bleeding out everywhere," Lorcan said. "He was going to give us away with a trail if we weren't careful."

I lifted my eyebrows at Lorcan. "You're such a bleeding heart."

He shrugged. "Only for people who deserve it."

Considering those guys had brought down the chopper and killed Jonathan, I thought he probably had a point.

"But you didn't come across Hollan?"

"Nope. And we've been on every level now. This was our last one. We came across more of his guys—each casing the place in pairs, but we took them down."

"So where the hell is he? Do you think he just left?" I hated the possibility that he may have slipped through our fingers yet again. I needed this to all come to an end.

Isaac shook his head. "I have no idea, but we need to get everyone out of here. This place isn't safe."

"We've left Kingsley and Devlin in the control room," Alex said. "Devlin's still cuffed to that chair."

Isaac's lips thinned. "We'll take the chair with us, if we have to."

"Let's stick to the stairs," Lorcan said. "Something about this doesn't feel right."

"I know what you mean."

We hurried to the staircase. Isaac and Alex led the way. The boys were right behind them, moving as a pack. Then it was me with my aunt, followed by Lorcan and Clay.

"Keep going, sugar," Clay said, glancing over his shoulder to the door we'd just entered by. He clearly thought there was a chance we might be followed. "I've got your back."

I was glad he did.

As a now large group, we continued up the stairs, leaving one floor behind us, then the next, decreasing the distance between us and the outside world. My thighs burned with the exertion, and my breath grew tight in my lungs. I didn't want to be down here any longer. I had a bad feeling about this place, as though our moments here were numbered.

From somewhere in the walls came a crackling noise, and then a voice came over the intercom. "I know you can hear me."

I froze, my heart lurching, instantly recognizing who the voice belonged to.

Hollan. That son of a bitch.

Hollan's voice continued, blaring from the walls. "If you want to see your boss alive again, and the black guy, too, I suggest you all come up to the control room right now." There was a pause, and then he added, "And yes, Darcy, I'm talking about you, too."

We each exchanged a glance. Shit.

My stomach cramped with anxiety. I'd known this was all running too smoothly. Something was bound to have gone wrong. Now Hollan was up in the control room with Devlin and Kingsley. Devlin was cuffed, and Kingsley was hurt. I didn't know how Hollan had managed to sneak back in there. Perhaps he'd been hiding there all along, biding his time, and waiting to make his move.

"Fuck," Lorcan swore. "We've combed this place. Where the hell has he been, the coward?"

Isaac shook his head. "He lost too many men, so he's just been hiding while we searched this place? That's an all-time low, even for him."

But hiding and taking Kingsley and Devlin hostage meant Hollan was desperate. He didn't have any men left, and we far outnumbered him. Didn't that mean we'd won? The boys and my aunt were hopefully going to be safe now.

But no, he had Kingsley and Devlin, which meant he still had one over on us. I knew we shouldn't have left them.

"Can my aunt take the boys out of here?" I asked. "Is there an exit to the outside world if they keep going up?"

Isaac nodded. "Yeah, the escape route. It's a hatch, like the one where the elevator is, only without the car. It's only accessible from the inside. You'll need a code—four, eight, nine, nine—to get out. I guess I don't need to ask you if you'll remember the number?"

Lorcan lifted a hand. "Wait, she can't go with them. Hollan wants her there, too."

Isaac's lips thinned. "The moment we see Hollan, we'll put a hole in his head. I'm sick of the son of a bitch's games. This ends now."

"But he wants Darcy there," Lorcan insisted. "What if he kills Devlin or Kingsley the moment he doesn't see her?"

"Lorcan is right," I agreed. "I've always felt this was personal between me and Hollan. I've known the man since I was a child. He killed my father. How could I not think it was personal? He obviously feels the same way."

Clay folded his arms across his chest, his stormy eyes darkening with anger. "So we just give him what he wants? We give him Darcy? Are you fucking kidding me right now?"

"We're not giving him Darcy," Isaac said. "We're all right there. There's no way he can win this. It's seven against one."

The angry glare of Clay's eyes didn't lessen. "Unless he has a whole army he's going to bring down on our heads."

"We took care of the men aboveground, and the ones he brought down here."

"As far as we know," I pointed out.

"We have to go," Isaac said. "We can't abandon Kingsley and Devlin."

He was right. There was no way any of us would do that.

"Let's get Sarah and the boys to safety first." I handed Sarah my gun. She must have left the one she'd had down at the gun range. "I don't think you're going to need it, but just in case. Run for the tree line and wait for us there, okay?"

"Come with us, Darcy," she pleaded.

I shook my head. "I'm sorry, I can't."

"Please."

"Take the boys and get out of here and hide. Can you do that?"

Her gaze searched my face. "What if he sees us?"

"We won't let him see you. That's what we'll be doing. We'll be dealing with him, once and for all."

She stared at me, and I saw the anguish in her eyes, how she wanted to grab me and drag me with her, while knowing I'd never do anything I didn't want to. My stubbornness was even worse than hers. I guessed it ran in the family.

I pulled her to me and gave her a squeeze. "We'll be with you soon. Just look after the boys until then, okay? Then this will all be over."

I knew it was a big ask, but my heart was torn between making sure Kingsley was safe, and wanting my aunt to be reassured. I didn't have feelings for Devlin, but I knew they all looked up to him, and anything that would hurt these men would hurt me, too.

"What's the code to release the hatch?" I asked her, wanting to make sure she knew it.

"Four, eight, nine, nine."

"Right." The numbers danced around my vision. "Now, go."

She gave me a final glance, and then ushered the boys up the final set of stairs. We waited until we heard a beep, and then a gust of cool, fresh air filtered down into the stairwell. I wished we'd done more for them, and I prayed they'd all be safe out there now. Maybe we could have sent a couple of the guys to help protect them, but then what if they were perfectly safe—they were the ones who had escaped, after all—and it was Kingsley and Devlin who suffered the punishment of us not all turning up, despite Hollan's instructions?

"Okay, let's do this," Isaac said.

We went to the door Alex and I had initially come through when we'd left the control room.

Pushing through, I took a moment to piece together what I was seeing.

Devlin was still in the chair, and, in a second chair beside him, was Kingsley. He looked furious, his neck sinking into his bulked shoulders, reminding me of that half bull, half man creature, the Minotaur. Behind him stood Hollan, and, as I'd pretty much expected, he pressed the muzzle of a gun into the back of Kingsley's head.

"Don't you dare hurt ..." I began, but then my words trailed away. Something else had caught my eye, and I realized both Kingsley and Devlin were looking that way, too. All eyes were glued on the screens which surrounded us. Automatically, I followed their gazes.

They were no longer blank.

I gasped and clamped my hand to my mouth.

There, multiplied over and over on the screens, were the same live images.

We were looking at the boys Hollan had taken. Metal circles were around their wrists, the circles attached to chains, and the chains all attached to another hoop embedded into the concrete floor. A couple of the younger boys were crying, the older ones trying to comfort them, while looking close to tears themselves.

"Oh, my God."

Isaac lifted his gun, pointing it directly at Hollan. "Don't move a muscle."

Hollan laughed. "You don't think you're in the position to give orders, do you?"

But Isaac didn't lower his gun, and kept it pointed right at Hollan.

"Where are they?" I demanded. "What have you done to them? I swear to God, if you've hurt them ..."

"The boys are fine. Scared, as you can see, but otherwise physically unharmed. They won't be for long, though. That space they're in is going to start to fill with water within a matter of hours. It's cold water, too, ice cold. They'll feel it through every inch of their bones. But not for long, because if I'm not there to free them, they're going to drown."

"You fucking bastard." Glancing back to the video footage of the boys on the screen, my heart twisted with pain. One of the boys appeared to be significantly younger than the other two, and I knew that must be Tad. They looked terrified. Why would Hollan do such a thing? Were they being kept somewhere near? It was impossible to tell from the footage.

"So, you see," he lifted the hand not holding the gun in a 'what can you do' gesture, "you really don't have any choice but to let me walk right out of here. And don't think you can find the boys and free them yourselves. Like I said, they're on borrowed time, and besides, I have a backup. No one will be able to free them, even if they happen to come across them." He looked directly at me. "I thought what I did was rather poetic. It's almost a shame I won't get to show it off, because after all, you have a good mind for dates, don't you, Darcy?

What the fuck was that supposed to mean?"

"It doesn't matter what you've set up." Isaac's lips had thinned, and he was shaking his head. "I'm not going to let you walk. Not again. You've walked away from this one too many times, and you keep turning up like a bad case of shingles."

I looked to the others, panicked. Was Isaac going to shoot him anyway? If he did, we'd never find the boys. They needed to step in.

"Clay, Alex, do something," I begged.

They both gave me helpless looks. I didn't bother to beg Lorcan—I recognized the cold fury on his face, and knew he'd probably back up Isaac's desire to shoot him anyway.

"Isaac, please, look at the children. Those boys, they're the same as the ones you know here. Don't let them die for this son of a bitch. We'll catch up with him again, just like we've always done."

Isaac ignored me. "Why are you doing this?" he growled at Hollan. "What the hell are you hoping to achieve?"

Hollan gave a cold laugh. "The end of all of you, for a start. But you already *are* over, you just haven't realized it yet. You were over the moment I got my hands on the memory stick and was able to spread its contents throughout most of the FBI, and police departments, and even the government. You're not a secret anymore."

"So you've won," Isaac replied. "It's over. That doesn't mean we're going to let you walk away. Numerous men, including Darcy's father, are dead because of you. You have to pay for that."

He shrugged. "You make me pay, and you'll be making those four innocent boys pay, too. I was always going to have a backup plan to ensure I'd be able to walk out of here unharmed. That my backup plan also happens to cause you pain is just an added bonus."

Isaac's green eyes narrowed. "What did we ever do to you to make you hate us so much?"

He gave a cold laugh. "I think Devlin can answer that one, can't you, Devlin?" He looked back to Isaac. "Maybe you need to talk to your boss a little more, rather than blaming everything on me."

The atmosphere suddenly changed, ice prickling through the air, like hot water thrown into sub-zero temperatures.

"What are you talking about?" Isaac snarled.

Hollan glanced back up at the screen, but he was addressing Devlin again now. "You act as though you're doing those kids a favor, but you're raising them to be nothing more than machines to do your bidding."

Devlin shook his head. "That's not true."

"Bullshit. This is all over for you and your kind. The moment I got hold of those coordinates, it was all over."

"So let the boys go," Devlin said. "We'll have to disband now, anyway. What do you think you're going to gain by doing this?"

"I'll get to punish you. You and that bitch's father turned against me all those years ago. We had a plan, and you destroyed it."

A jolt of confusion hit me. "What?"

Now it was my turn to be the focus of Hollan's attention. "How do you think your father got hold of the coordinates? I was the one who managed to get them uploaded to that memory stick, and then your father went and encrypted it."

"How did you even get the coordinates to upload them?"

"Your friend here, Devlin, got an access code. He didn't want to be pinpointed, so he gave it to me."

A flash of panic swept across Devlin's face.

Isaac took a step forward, and the direction of his gun wavered between Hollan and Devlin. "What's he talking about, Devlin?"

Urgency joined the panic in Devlin's expression. "I never thought it was a good idea that we didn't know the locations of the bases. It seemed pointless to me. I argued it over and over, but no one would give in. I knew Hollan, and your father, too, Darcy. Hollan told me he'd be able to hack the server to get the coordinates, but when he did that and uploaded them onto the memory stick, your father wiped the data and encrypted the drive."

"So you killed him!" I stared at Devlin, aghast.

"No! Never. I had nothing to do with that. That was all Hollan. I only wanted to know the locations of the other bases. Considering my position in the organization, I thought I had the right to know."

I shook my head, unable to believe what I was hearing, but at the same time, knowing it was the truth.

Devlin continued, as though he hoped he could talk his way out of this situation and back into all our favors. "Hollan was the one who killed your father and took the stick. I had nothing to do with it. It was only after he told me what he'd done that I realized what kind of man I was dealing with."

"But you played your part in my father's death? If you hadn't wanted those coordinates, he'd still be alive today." I was shaking my head, barely conscious that I was doing so, my body not wanting to believe what my ears were hearing. I'd trusted this man, thought he was on our side, when all along he'd colluded with Hollan.

A hand on my arm, steadying me. Isaac. I looked to him, my eyes wide. "Did you know about this?" I whirled to the others. "Did all of you know about this?"

"No, Darcy. No. This is as much news to us as it is to you. We had no idea Devlin was behind the memory stick containing the coordinates getting into Hollan's hands."

I had to believe them. I had to. Not believing them was simply unthinkable.

Hollan laughed. "So now you know the truth. And time is ticking away. The longer you keep me here talking, the less time I'm going to have to release those boys before that spot starts filling with water."

We all stared, aghast at the sudden revelations, unsure what to do. Even the guys seemed knocked off balance, discovering the man they'd looked up to most of their lives wasn't that same person they'd believed in.

"So, you give me your word that I can walk out of here, unharmed?" Hollan pressed.

Isaac wouldn't even look at him. Instead, he stared at the screen, watching the frightened faces of those boys. Then he nodded—an almost imperceptible motion. "I give you my word."

A wide smile spread cross Hollan's face, and fury swelled up inside of me. There was nothing I could do.

Hollan lowered his weapon. "Good."

He turned his back to head toward the elevator.

In one swift movement, Isaac lifted his gun. Two shots rang out, and I screamed, the sound piercing my ears. Hollan took one staggered step, reaching out as though he might be able to grab hold of something for purchase, and then fell flat to his stomach. Two bullet holes bloomed red in the back of his jacket. I clutched my hand to my mouth as Isaac left my side and crossed over to him.

"I lied," he told Hollan as he lifted his gun once more and put a third hole in the back of Hollan's head.

Chapter Eighteen

Time stood still.

We were all rooted in place, staring at Hollan's body. There was no coming back from that. Hollan was as dead as it was possible to get.

I managed to tear my vision from Hollan, and glance to the screens covering the walls.

"Oh, my God." I spoke between my fingers, my hand still clamped to my mouth.

Isaac had just killed the one person who knew the boys' location.

"What have you done?"

His jaw was tensed. "What needed to be done. We couldn't trust him to let the boys go free, anyway."

"He might have told us where they were!"

Isaac's eyebrows lifted. "You believe that? You knew him better than anyone." He shot Devlin a glare. "Or so we thought."

Devlin shook his head. "I'm sorry. It was a long time ago."

"You should have told us!"

"And then you'd never have taken another order from me ever again."

The rigidness from Isaac's face didn't fade. "Yeah, and maybe then we wouldn't be in this mess."

Lorcan stormed forward, his weapon pointed at Devlin's head. "You gave that bastard access to the locations. You started all of this six years ago. You were the one who got Darcy's dad killed."

My stomach flipped at the truth of his words.

Devlin shook his head. "I knew I'd done wrong. I've been trying to fix it ever since."

"How?" Lorcan spat. "By using us to get the code and the memory stick? All because your ego needed some massaging?"

"That wasn't how it was. I thought I was doing the right thing at the time."

Kingsley stood, his hand clutched to his ribs. "Bullshit. If you'd thought that, you'd never have used Hollan in the first place to try to hide your actions."

Devlin dropped his chin to his chest, and his shoulders shook with silent sobs. "I'm sorry. I'm so very sorry."

He looked like a broken man, and Lorcan slowly lowered his weapon.

Clay's arm hooked around my shoulders and he pulled me against him and kissed the top of my head. I exhaled a sigh from the deepest part of my lungs and sagged against him. Hollan was dead. Finally. And Devlin had conspired with him years ago to get access to the locations of the bases. And I had given the coordinates right to him. My mind was spinning, partly out of relief, partly confusion, but also with fear that this wasn't over.

Not yet.

"We can't fight about this now," I said. "We need to figure out where Hollan has those boys chained up."

We all looked back to the screen, horrified, as the live feed continued. If we didn't find those children, they were going to die.

Isaac sat at one of the computers linked to the screens, and his fingers flew over the keyboard. "It's a longshot, but I might be able to pinpoint where the feed is coming from."

I nodded. "Good." Even a longshot was something at this point.

"How many of his men are still alive?" Alex asked. "We could question them. Maybe someone knows something."

Lorcan shook his head, his jaw tensed. "Most of them are dead, and the two we tied up in the kitchen said they didn't know what had happened to the boys, just that they'd been taken away."

"We could bring them up and see if we can get more out of them," Alex suggested.

"If they don't know anything more," Lorcan said, "then we'll only be wasting time."

Devlin yanked at the cuffs. "Let me go. Hollan has the keys to the handcuffs. I can help."

"No fucking chance." Isaac didn't forgive so easily.

I didn't blame him. I didn't want Devlin anywhere near us right at that moment either. I was surprised one of the guys—Lorcan or Isaac, in particular—hadn't already shot him. I guessed after all these years, they still felt some loyalty toward him.

Kingsley stepped in, lifting his hand, though his handsome features were steeped in pain. I had the horrible feeling he might have cracked a rib or two when we'd crashed. "Wait. There were things Hollan said. Things we already know. The water level is going to change in a couple of hours, and he said the water is cold. It has to be somewhere between here and Atlanta. He wouldn't have had time to take them anywhere else, and it's going to be within a couple of hours of here, or he wouldn't have made it there in time himself."

"Unless he got someone else to do it," Alex pointed out.

"True, but Hollan isn't a man—*wasn't* a man—who delegates easily. I don't know if he'd have trusted someone else to do it. What if the other person or people were too soft and the boys got to them? He wouldn't take that risk."

Isaac twisted from the computer. "Kingsley's right. Do we have a map?"

Kingsley swept the space beneath the central console and retrieved a folded paper map. He unfolded it and spread it out across the console. "Okay," he said. "The Atlanta base is here." He jabbed his finger against the paper. "And if Hollan thinks he could reach the boys within a couple of hours, then they must be located within that journey time."

I thought of all the time we'd wasted at the second base, while he'd been locking those poor kids up in some kind of concrete dungeon.

We pored over the map, studying it.

"There must be water nearby," Clay said, frowning.

I glanced at him. "A lake, or a river?"

"Something tidal?" Alex suggested.

But the location would be nowhere near the coast.

"Shit." Clay locked his hands in his hair as he thought. "We know there's a building, and the concrete suggests something industrial."

We fixed our attention on the map again, concentrating on the area two hours between here and Atlanta. Numerous blue lines curved through the topography, some thicker than others.

I spotted something. "What about there?" I pointed to the map. The square block was barely a dot. "What is it?"

Kingsley frowned down. "A waste water management facility."

"Could that be the place?"

We looked at each other, hopeful, expectant.

Isaac straightened and stepped closer to the screens. The boys were shivering and hugging each other, the younger boy's shoulders jerking as he cried, Isaac moved between the screens, studying them, even though each one was identical. His focus was intent, and I noticed the other guys watching him, too, waiting for him to make the next move.

"There." He pointed at something on screen. "What's that?"

As one, we all moved forward to join him. On the metal ring, secured into the concrete floor, which all of the children were attached to, were the initials J.T.

"What's the name of the company?" Isaac asked.

I double checked. "Johnson and Turner Industries."

The initials fit.

Kingsley looked between us expectantly. "So it's the right place?"

Isaac nodded. "Yeah, it's the right place." He frowned and leaned in toward the screens again. "We have another problem, though."

I didn't like the sound of that.

Isaac pointed at the ring on screen that held the chains for each of the boys. "Look, that's a combination lock."

I stared at him. "What does that mean?"

"That when Hollan was talking about having a backup, he meant that. We don't know the code to unlock it, even if we get to the boys on time."

My mouth dropped open. "Can we take something with us to cut the metal?"

"We're going to have to, but it'll be slow going trying to cut through something that thick, and if it's already submerged, we're going to have more than a problem."

"Shit. Shit. Shit."

Isaac stepped away from the screens. "We can't waste any more time."

We burst into movement, scooping up weapons and heading for the elevator.

"Hey!" Devlin yelled, banging up and down in his chair, rocking it back and forth. "You can't leave me like this."

No one bothered to justify his request with a comment. He should have been pleased he was still alive. I was surprised the guys had left him that way, considering what he'd just admitted to, but maybe they figured Devlin deserved to be tried as a traitor rather than killed.

My mind whirled at the thought of the fallout from all of this. What would happen to everyone? It wasn't as though a secret organization could continue when it was no longer secret. And Hollan said he'd released the locations of the bases. Anyone could find them now. Everything was going to have to change, but I had no idea where that would leave everyone. I'd thought I had a new home with the guys, a new job, even, but the dream of that was over now. There was no job anymore.

Now wasn't the time to start lamenting about my future. We still needed to rescue those boys. I prayed we'd be in time—not only for the lives of the boys, but for Isaac, too. I understood why he'd shot Hollan, but if we didn't get to them, he'd blame himself for their deaths, and, in a way, he would be partially responsible. Different choices could have been made, which would result in a different outcome. Isaac was far from stupid. None of us said it out loud, but we all understood the reality.

But I wasn't going to pretend I wasn't happy Lyle Hollan was dead. I wished I'd been the one to pull the trigger myself, but instead Isaac had done that for me. He'd shouldered that responsibility on my behalf, and though it had shocked me, I was grateful to him for doing it.

We crammed into the elevator, shoulder to shoulder, our weapons pressed between us. I hoped our days of needing to be armed at all times had come to an end with the death of Hollan, but I understood the need to be cautious. Isaac still had a bloodied head and arms from the helicopter crash, and I didn't miss the way Kingsley winced every time he moved. It hurt me to see them in pain, but before we could take care of their injuries, we needed to make sure everyone was safe.

The doors opened, and I blinked in surprise.

Night had fallen since we'd been underground. I hadn't given any thought to what time it might have been, but it seemed the day had passed.

It was pitch black now. Only the circle of a full moon hanging low in the sky and the winking of stars gave us any light. The men around me tensed, muscles hardening, breath catching in lungs. Hollan might be dead, but there was still the chance some of his men might be around to continue his fight. But all remained quiet, so we edged out of the elevator, the men remaining close, creating a protective shield around me. I'd given my gun to Aunt Sarah, and I looked for her now, trying to pick her out in the dark. The hatch to the stairs didn't open up here, but would have been farther away, closer to the tree line. I'd told her to hide, so I assumed that was what she was doing until she knew we were safe.

I wanted to call to her, but for the moment I kept my mouth shut. I didn't want to alert anyone to our presence unnecessarily, and I knew the guys were still scoping the area, making sure Hollan's men were either dead or gone. Calling out to my aunt would be like putting a flashing beacon above our heads.

We edged forward, starting to spread out. Clay's hand wrapped around my waist and he pulled me toward him.

"Stay with me," he said, his voice low.

I nodded. Unprotected, with no weapon of my own, I felt unexpectedly helpless. A few weeks ago, I wouldn't have given a second thought about not being armed, but now it felt as though I was walking around naked.

A cough came from my right, and then the sound of someone being shushed. The others heard it, too, each of us freezing and turning in that direction. But no shots were fired. Nothing to make us think we were being attacked.

"Sarah?" I hissed into the night.

"Darcy?" a small voice came back.

I looked to the others, asking them if it was safe without saying a word. Isaac nodded, and I allowed myself to breathe.

The hulk of the remains of the helicopter lay like a dinosaur, collapsed and dying. I pictured Jonathan's body still lying inside. He'd been a decent man, and he hadn't deserved to die like that. We'd have to make sure any family was notified and that he was given a good burial.

The shape of my aunt rushed out from between the trees. Hurrying along behind her, like ducklings chasing a mother duck, were the boys, the older ones leading the way, the smaller kids sticking close to the sides of the bigger boys. I wondered what would happen to them now.

I wasn't the only one whose life was about to completely change, and it would hit them far harder than it would me.

"Are you okay?" Sarah asked as she reached me. Though the light was dim, I could see her checking me over, looking for any injuries.

I nodded. "I'm fine. I promise. What about you and the boys? Everyone safe?"

"Yes, thank God."

We pulled each other into a tight hug, and I forced myself to let go, knowing we couldn't waste any more time.

"Is he ..." she started to ask.

"He's dead, Aunt Sarah. The man who killed Dad is dead."

Her lips pressed together, containing her emotion. She gave a sharp nod. "Good."

"There's something we still have to do," I told her. "We have to go and get some of the other boys. They're all alone. They need us. Can you take one of the vans and drive this group back to our house? I'll be there as soon as I can."

She nodded. "Are you going to be okay?"

"Yes, I'll be fine. Hollan's dead. This is almost over. We just need to make sure the other boys are safe."

She lowered her voice. "Where's Devlin?"

My shoulders stiffened. "He's alive. We left him still handcuffed down there."

"What? Why?" Shock registered on her face.

"He'd colluded with Hollan all those years ago, so Hollan could get him the coordinates for all the locations. He thought he had a right to know, but in doing so let them get into Hollan's hands. If it hadn't been for Dad taking the memory stick and putting the code on it, both of them would have known the coordinates years ago."

"So Devlin knew Hollan was the one who killed your father? And he did nothing?"

"He wanted to get the memory stick back, but he knew it was no use without the code. I guess he was worried Hollan was going to expose him or thought they'd get hold of the code one day, which I guess is where I came in."

She brought her fingers to her lips. "Jesus."

I shook my head, turmoil churning up inside me. "I gave it right to him."

She touched my arm, trying to offer me some comfort. "You had no way of knowing, Darcy. You were doing what you thought was right at the time."

I sucked in a deep breath, trying to control my emotions.

"We gotta go, Darc," Alex called to me.

I glanced over to where the guys were waiting and nodded. "Yeah, I'm coming."

"We'll talk more later, okay, when all this is done? I'll meet you back at the house."

"I want to go with Isaac and Clay," one of the boys cried.

"We'll be with you soon, buddy," Clay said. "Be good for Sarah, okay? It'll be a couple of hours, and then we'll all be back together again."

My aunt gave me a final hug then gestured for the boys to follow her down the hill, toward where the vehicles were parked. We'd be going that way, too, needing to get ourselves on the road and toward the place we believed the boys were being held. I had to believe we were right about the location. Being wrong didn't bear thinking about.

We wanted to move faster, but were cautious of Kingsley and possibly broken ribs. But knowing time was running out pushed us on. Alex helped Kingsley, supporting him with a shoulder under his armpit, Kingsley's arm around his neck. We needed to watch our footing, too. In the dark, the numerous pieces of rusted machinery from when this place was a working forestry still lay around, and it would be easy to go over on an ankle. We didn't need any more injuries right now.

We reached the vans. I had the horrible thought that Hollan might have sabotaged them before entering the base, preventing any possible escapees. The idea made me nauseated. What would we do then? We were a couple of hours away, and there was no way we'd reach the boys in time. It wasn't as though we could just call an Uber out here. But then I realized Hollan's vehicles must be around here someplace. His men had had to arrive in something. They must have been parked somewhere beneath the canopy of the trees, hidden from our approaching view when we'd been in the helicopter.

But, despite my fears, Isaac located the keys beneath the visor of one of the vehicles, and within minutes we'd all piled in and the engine was running.

I only hoped we'd get there in time.

Chapter Nineteen

Isaac drove as fast as he dared, his fingers tight around the steering wheel, his knuckles white. I wanted to put my hand on his arm or shoulder, try to offer him some kind of comfort, but I didn't want to remove his attention from the road.

We swapped the paper map for the more high-tech Sat-Nav on Isaac's laptop. He'd handed it to me as soon as we'd climbed in, and I now sat with it balanced on my lap, staring at the screen and willing the miles away. I wished there had been a way of getting the feed of the boys linked to this computer so we could at least have seen them. Leaving them, even though it was only on a video feed, felt like a strange kind of abandonment.

Now that we were no longer expecting to be attacked at any moment, Alex took the time to check Kingsley over properly. Kingsley was able to lie across the back seat, though he still needed to have his legs bent and his neck propped up against the opposite side—like a grown man trying to sleep in a toddler bed.

"I don't think they're broken," Alex said after checking him over. "You might have some fractures, but that's impossible for me to tell without an X-ray. I'll strap them up, and that should give you some relief."

"Thanks," Kingsley growled, wincing with pain.

"I've got some painkillers, too. They'll help take the edge off."

"Nothing too strong," Kingsley said. "I need my head clear."

Clay leaned back in his seat. "You think we can't pull this off without your brains, Kingsley?"

"That's exactly what I think."

Clay snorted, and I tried to smile. I wanted to relax, but the faces of those poor boys kept appearing in my head. I hated to think of how terrified they must be—to be kidnapped and then held in such conditions. I remembered George's description of them and placed their names to the faces in my mind—the youngest, Tad, at only six, and Scott and Xander at eleven, and Chris, who was the oldest boy at twelve years old.

I hoped George was all right with Andrea and the boys from the second base. At some point, I hoped we'd all be able to be reunited and figure out what came next, but that would be a whole different meeting if we didn't make it to the boys in time.

My stomach curdled with anger toward a dead man. How could anyone do that? I'd always known he was a bastard, but using children to try to secure his getaway was the lowest of the low.

The van ate away the miles. We left the smaller roads and ended up on the freeway. I prayed there wouldn't be any accidents or traffic. The late hour meant the roads were quiet, and Isaac pushed the van as fast as he could. Two hours had passed since Hollan had told us the boys only had a matter of hours, and I feared we would be too late.

"There!" Lorcan pointed to an exit.

Isaac took it, swerving the vehicle hard enough that we all had to lean to the side to prevent ourselves being thrown.

"How far now?" Clay asked.

"Thirty minutes, at the most."

Anxiety coiled at my gut, and I leaned forward, my fingers hooking over the seat in front, gripping it tight. What if we were too late? What if we were in the wrong place? The thought of finding those boys' bodies and knowing we could have done something about it made me feel sick. I wasn't sure how any of us would live with ourselves, but in particular I was worried about Isaac. He was the one who'd pulled the trigger and ended Hollan's life, when he could have let him go. It was true,

Hollan may not have even freed the boys, and might have once more walked free with no repercussions, but we'd never know for sure.

The road we were on narrowed. Ahead of us, the shapes of buildings rose into the night sky. Big, ugly, concrete structures.

"We're close to the river," Alex said, leaning forward in his seat.

"That's a good sign, right?" I said hopefully.

"Let's hope so."

Isaac slowed the van to a crawl as we approached the water treatment plant. A high, chain link fence ran around the concrete buildings, with signs to stay out attached at regular intervals. Floodlights lit the grounds. I guessed this place ran twenty-four hours a day.

Isaac pulled the van to a halt, and we jumped out. We'd brought a hacksaw from the base, hoping to use it to cut through the combination lock, and Clay grabbed it from the back. A rancid stench filled the air, and we all covered our noses with hands or the tops of our shirts. The rush of a river on the other side filtered through to our ears.

"We've got to get in there."

The place was big—far bigger than I'd been expecting. How the hell were we supposed to find four small boys in a place this size?

At first I'd thought the place looked deserted, but then there was movement from the other side of the chain link fence. Each of us froze, and I saw the men reach for their weapons. I still felt bereft without my gun. I should have picked up a replacement, but I'd been too caught up in wanting to reach the boys quickly. Anyway, I hoped we wouldn't need it. Now that Hollan was taken care of, we were safe. It was only the boys who weren't.

A security guard came running over. He looked to be in his fifties, with a receding hairline and hollow cheeks. "Hey, what do you think you're doing? This is private property."

Isaac flashed him the badge, the same ID he'd shown to Andrea. There was no way the guard understood what it meant, but it looked official, and that was enough to grab his attention. "I need you to open up."

The guard frowned. "Why? What's happening?"

"We have reason to believe you have children on your premises who are in danger. If you don't let us in, you're going to have their blood on your hands."

Panic flitted across the guard's face. "Kids? I ain't seen no kids around here."

"Just do as I say."

The guard took a bunch of keys off his belt and got to work unlocking the padlock which hooked a chain from the gate to the fence. It rattled, the metal clinging together as the chain fell open, and the gate swung wide.

Isaac stepped through, leading the way, and the rest of us followed. The guard stared at us with wide, shocked eyes, clearly with no idea of what was going on and why all these people had turned up in the middle of the night.

"What's your name?" Isaac asked him.

"Tony Ferrera," he replied, his eyes darting between us.

"Listen to me, Tony" Isaac said. He always had a way of getting people to pay attention to him, to take him seriously. "We have reason to believe there are four children on the property and they're in extreme danger. Their lives are at risk. Do you understand what I'm saying to you?"

"I ain't seen no children!" he repeated.

Isaac ignored him. "A man named Lyle Hollan brought them here earlier—or it's possible he had someone else do it. Either way, it doesn't matter. We've seen live footage of the boys, and they're here, but they're chained up somewhere that's going to fill with water shortly, if it hasn't already. It's made of concrete, and has curved walls. Can you think of anywhere here that fits that description?"

Confusion flooded the man's face. "Err ... I don't know ..."

"Think, please!" I begged him. "Children's lives are in danger!"

He scrubbed his hand across the top of his head and looked around as though the answer might appear in midair. "Well, water's moving around this place all the time, but the main pipes are always full, so no one would be able to be inside them. The overflow pipe is mostly empty, though. They get flushed out once a day, about this time."

We glanced at each other.

"Curved walls and concrete could easily be the bottom of a pipe. That must be it," Isaac said. "Show us where it is."

The guard nodded then turned and took off at a run. We followed him, each of us jogging, though I glanced back toward Kingsley and could see he was in pain. He didn't complain, though, and I had to stop myself from reaching out and squeezing him.

The stench of the place grew stronger. The running made me want to breathe hard, but I limited myself to shallow breaths.

"We have to go inside to access it," said the guard. "It's this way." He'd stopped at the front of a square building, nowhere near as big as the main part of the plant. A heavy metal door barred the way, but he reached to grab his keys and unlocked it.

"What's that noise?" I asked.

The sound of water rushing deep beneath our feet.

"The pipes are being cleared out already," he said.

Oh, God, no. Were we too late?

The building housed equipment and a hole in the ground which had a ladder descending into it.

Isaac glanced at the equipment. "Is it possible to shut off the water?"

Tony shook his head. "No, it's too late now. It's already started."

"Shit."

"We have to get down there," I cried.

We didn't wait any longer. Isaac, Lorcan, and Clay went first, and I followed, climbing down, hand over foot, trying to move fast enough.

I dropped down, and the shock of ice cold water hit me. It was already up to my thighs. How much give had the boys had on the ends of those chains? I tried to remember. If they were tied too tightly, they might be submerged already.

Behind me, Kingsley, Alex, and the security guard dropped into the water. The guard had a flashlight and used it to illuminate the way. We had flashlights on our phones as well, and soon the huge pipe was lit with several swathes of light. I didn't know how long the phones would last with all this water around.

I looked around, desperately trying to spot some sign of the boys. We were in a large, concrete cylinder, about eight feet high, but I saw no sign of the children.

"Chris!" I yelled, my voice hollow in the tight space, bouncing back at me from the top of the water. "Tad? Scott? Xander?"

I listened hard, my ears straining. But there was nothing.

My heart sank, and angry, frustrated tears bit at the backs of my eyes.

Then a faint cry came back to us. "Help!"

"Oh, God."

Tony gasped. "Jesus Christ, there really is someone down here."

I wanted to comment that we weren't exactly doing this for fun, but figured now wasn't the time for smart-assed remarks.

We all hurried. The force of the water behind pushed us forward. Ice cold, nipping at my skin, threatening to steal my breath and take the feeling away from my limbs. Feeling as though my feet were going to be swept out from under me, I reached out blindly. My fingers caught a forearm, and I glanced over to make out Clay's profile in the gloom.

Those kids were in the dark with the water rushing at them.

"We're coming!" I called out. "Just hang on."

Another cry of fear met our ears, followed by the sound of soft crying, barely distinguishable over the rush of water.

Automatically, everyone lifted their lights in that direction.

"There!"

A spot ahead was illuminated, but not by our lights, but by some other source. I could just make out the shapes of children in the water. We'd found them. "Hang on," I called out to them. "We're coming."

We reached the boys heads held barely above water level. They stared at us with a combination of fear and hope, wondering if we were there to help, or if we were connected to the man who'd brought them here.

Lights had been positioned high in the curve between the walls and the roof, and beside them were the red blink of cameras. That bastard. He'd positioned the lights, not so the boys would be able to see, but so the cameras would be able to film them.

The men went to help the boys. They'd been trying to swim, but the weight of the chains around their wrists had been pulling them under. They spluttered and fought, but then calmed and allowed the guys to hold them up.

"The man left us here," the oldest managed between gulps for breath. "He took us and he chained us up."

"I know." Isaac wedged his shoulder under Chris's arm. "You don't need to worry about him anymore. We're here to help you."

The youngest boy, Tad, was the weakest by far, and Clay scooped him up, supporting his chin with one hand, so the boy's face was above water. "You're okay. We've got you. You're safe now."

But they weren't safe yet. We still had to get the ring open to unhook their chains.

"You need to cut the ring," I told Clay. "Let me take Tad."

Clay nodded, and we swapped places. Kingsley moved in to help, though he was still struggling with his own pain. The security guard stood off to one side, looking baffled about what was happening.

Clay sucked in a deep breath then ducked beneath the water with the hacksaw. It seemed so basic, but it was all we had.

But in less than a minute, he shot back up again. "It's not working. The water means I can't get any traction. The saw is having no effect whatsoever."

"Shit."

The water was getting higher. It wouldn't be long before the length of the chains would force the boys under.

The lock. The number. What had Hollan said about it? That I was good with dates. Was that what he was hinting at, that the number for the combination lock was a date that I would remember? He'd said it was almost poetic, that he was disappointed he wouldn't be able to show it off.

That feeling about this being personal hit me all over again.

My lifeline appeared in front of me. In the gloom, I watched all the important dates of my life flash in a row of boxes, curving away from me, to my left. My birthdays, my graduation, and, closer to me, so appearing larger, were the recent events—the date Isaac and the others took me. I zoomed in on each of them, trying to figure out if any of them could be the numbers Hollan was talking about. Then I focused on one date which, even though it was years ago, now appeared larger in my vision and seemed to have taken on a glow in the dim light.

The date my dad died.

No, the date Hollan murdered my father.

I gasped. "I think I know the numbers!"

Chapter Twenty

"Here," I said to Clay. "Help me with him."

I handed Tad over to Clay. On the other side, I could feel Kingsley struggling, not only with his ribs, but with whatever weakness had happened to his leg in the crash, and the cold of the water was making him unstable. Tad kicked his legs to try to stay afloat, but the movement was feeble. As the smallest of the boys, the cold had affected him the worst, and I knew if we dropped him he'd go under.

But I knew the numbers.

"Give me the flashlight." I didn't wait for a response, and just snatched it out of the security guard's hand.

The water was edging higher with every minute that passed. Trying not to think about what I was diving into—despite the guard insisting this was clean water they were flushing through—I took a deep breath and plunged beneath the surface.

The frigid water locked around my skull like a vise. It wasn't deep enough for me to need to swim. I forced my eyes open, the dark, murky water pressing against my eyeballs. I pointed the light in the direction of the ring and the combination lock. Everything was blurry, and I pushed myself closer, trying to get my vision to adjust. I'd never be able to get the right numbers if I couldn't even see them. My heart felt as though it had grown bigger, swelling in my chest and pounding against my rib cage. My lungs had started to burn as the oxygen levels in my blood began to fall.

The first number appeared in front of me, in its usual spot, but now suspended in the water. I reached for the combination lock, my fingers

161

numb from the cold, and scrolled until I'd hit that number. I went to the second digit and repeated the process. My lungs were on fire now, my whole chest feeling like it was going to burst. I knew I didn't have enough oxygen to stay down much longer.

Wretched, but desperate, I pushed upward, and the top of my head broke the surface. I gasped, the sound loud and painful. It was an incredible relief, though that relief didn't last long.

"You have to hurry, sugar!"

Clay was still holding Tad. The boy's chain had stretched as far as it could, and because the boy's arms were shorter than the others, he was barely reaching the surface. His eyes were squeezed shut, his face tilted backward in the water, only barely staying above.

Fuck.

I sucked in another breath and went back under. The sound of the water was hollow around my ears as I pushed deeper, back to the lock. I still had four numbers to go. My fingers felt fat as I scrolled, matching up the numbers on the lock to the digits that were floating around me. My lungs burned, the need to open my mouth and breathe screaming through me. I had to ignore it, though. I had to get this done. If I didn't, the little boy would drown, and soon the others would follow.

Finally, the last number scrolled into place, and the lock popped. I had to stop myself from crying out with relief, knowing it would only earn me a lungful of water. Fumbling frantically, desperate to not only pull the chains off the ring, but also to get to the surface, I yanked the chains off the ring, one by one. I had to pull the tension on the chains tight in order to be able to thread them through the gap, but then that tension vanished as soon as I released them, and I knew whichever boy was on the end would no longer be pulled beneath the surface.

The moment the final chain slid free, I used my feet to push up and burst to the surface. Coughing as the cold air filled my lungs once more, I wiped the water out of my eyes. I was cold down to the bone, shaking furiously.

"Well done, love," Isaac said, still holding one of the boys. The water was deep enough for them not to be able to touch now, even the older ones. "Let's get the hell out of here."

None of us needed any more encouragement.

The men gathered around me, supporting me where they could. Everyone was freezing, and the youngest boy, Tad, was still crying.

It felt like we'd never reach the ladder. For a moment, I thought this had been Hollan's final laugh, and he'd had someone shut us down in here, and we'd never find our way out, but then the guard called us over.

"We're here!"

Because it was dark outside, the entrance had been hard to see.

We helped each other up, one by one, stopping at the top to haul the next person up. It was important to get the boys out of the cold water, but the night was still chilly, and everyone was wet and shivering.

"I should call the cops," the guard said, but Isaac put out a hand to stop him.

"No need. We're better than the cops. We'll make sure the boys get to where they need to be."

I wasn't sure where that place would be now that the locations of the bases had been exposed, but I figured Isaac had some idea.

We made it back to the van. Alex found some blankets and a couple of changes of sweatshirts, and we each made do, drying ourselves off as best we could, while Clay ran the hot air. There weren't enough blankets or spare clothes to go around, so we shared a couple, and huddled in together to keep warm.

Do you know what happened to our friend?" one of the older boys, Chris, asked. "His name's George. We lost him after those men arrived and started shooting."

"He's safe," Isaac told him. "He's with another team. You'll be back together soon."

The boys exchanged relieved glances.

"What about the man who took us?" asked, the other boy, Xander. "The one who locked us up down there?"

"He's dead," Isaac replied. "You'll never have to worry about him again."

Chapter Twenty-one

I t was over.

Hollan was dead, and the boys were safe.

I didn't know what would happen now, but the relief of it made me lightheaded. Or perhaps that was just hypothermia.

When everyone was dried off and warmed up, we made sure the boys were strapped in, and then we left the premises. Alex had checked everyone over to make sure we didn't need any medical attention.

I'd left my aunt with the boys from our base, so it made sense that we headed back to D.C. I found myself longing to see my home again, something that surprised me. I'd spent so long apathetic toward the house and the life I had there, but now that was the only place I wanted to be.

Isaac would make contact with Andrea and hope she'd found the other bases safe. There would need to be a lot of meetings over the days and weeks to come, trying to figure out what would happen to all the people involved. Would they regroup and start again? I didn't know. All I knew was that I wanted to sleep for about three weeks, and then do nothing more exciting than watching Netflix and ordering in take-out food for the foreseeable future. I'd had enough excitement to last me a lifetime.

I dozed in the van on the drive back, my head on Clay's shoulder, while Lorcan sat on the other side of me, his fingers laced with mine. Alex sat back with the boys, keeping an eye on them to make sure none were showing any signs of hypothermia or shock. So far, so good, and other than being frightened and confused about what had happened, the boys appeared none the worse for their experience. Isaac drove, and Kingsley took the passenger seat, needing the space because of his ribs. He'd need medical attention at some point to check that nothing was broken, but for the moment all any of us wanted to do was get somewhere warm, dry, and safe.

I roused when we hit the outskirts of the city, my heart lifting. I'd forgotten how much I missed this place. Only a month or so ago I'd believed I'd hated the bright lights, and the Metro, and the people, and the damned Monument. Now I felt my soul lifting at the sight of it.

Home.

I wanted to see Aunt Sarah, too, and hold her tight, and tell her we'd made it, and thank her for everything she'd done. None of us had been perfect in our decisions over the past few weeks, but life was short, and I wasn't about to hold anything against her. I hoped the boys we'd put her in charge of hadn't run her off her feet. They might have continued with the subdued nature they'd been in when we left, or they might be giving her hell. It could easily go either way. At least they weren't strangers to her, though, and she knew how to handle them. Aunt Sarah had never been a pushover. She'd survived a teenaged me, after all.

Isaac knew the way from the time we'd been here before.

By the time we pulled up in front of the house, night had given way to day. We all climbed out, blinking in the diffused morning sunlight. Though I knew Hollan was dead, a part of me still churned with nerves, worrying we'd find something more than we'd anticipated, but everything looked quiet, and when I used my key to open the front door, a sleepy-looking Sarah was making her way down toward me in her robe.

Her face lit at the sight of me, and she held open her arms. I rushed forward, the men and boys at my back, and wrapped my arms around her. We held each other tight, and then she kissed my cheek.

"I'm so happy you're safe."

"Me, too," I said. "It's over."

She released me to look over my shoulder at the group behind me and smiled. "I think we're going to run out of beds."

"It doesn't matter. We can sleep anywhere. Everyone's exhausted." I looked around. "Where are the other boys?"

She gave a small laugh. "Where aren't they? In the spare room. In your room, too, Darcy. Some are on the floor. Everyone is safe, though, and that's all that matters."

I smiled at her. "Yes, you're right."

"Your clothes are damp," she said, touching my shoulder.

I nodded. "It's a long story, and I'm way too tired to tell it now."

"That's okay. Get yourself changed, and I'll try to find somewhere for everyone to sleep."

What I really wanted was to pull my five guys into a room and snuggle down with them all, like a bundle of affectionate cats, but I knew that wasn't going to be possible tonight—or at least today, as we'd already left night far behind us. We needed our rest, and with numerous people under one roof, it would be a case of making do.

Clean, dry clothes were handed out. We'd never completely gotten rid of my dad's stuff, and had only bagged it up and stored it away, so there was plenty of men's clothing to go around. It was too big for the boys, especially Tad, who wore the sweatshirt and pants comically, hanging off his small frame, but they were warm and dry and would do until we were all rested and could find something more suitable.

"I'm hungry," Tad said, his lower lip pouting.

"I don't have much," my aunt apologized. "We haven't been here in a while, so everything in the refrigerator turned and the bread looks like it's about to walk off on its own. I can do dried cereal, but that's about it."

The boy smiled. "Cereal is good. I like it better without milk anyway."

She returned the smile. "That's good, then, isn't it?"

The boys were practically asleep before they'd even finished eating. Clay lifted Tad, his eyes drooping, from the table and found him a spot on one of the couches. The adults were all hungry, too, but we could wait. Sleep was more important than food.

Sarah handed out spare pillows and blankets, and we all found a spot to bed down. The house resembled an emergency shelter after a natural disaster—a place of refuge. I found myself curled up with Clay on one side of me and Alex on the other. Kingsley had been given a camping mat because of his ribs, and was sleeping in the hall, and Isaac had taken up position near the front door. I noticed how he still kept his gun to hand. I thought we were safe here, but I figured it was just Isaac's natural stance to make sure his team was protected. Lorcan had copied his leader's position and rolled a mat down by the back door.

We were all here, we were all safe.

And with that being my last thought, I gave in to sleep.

⌘

I DIDN'T KNOW HOW MANY hours had passed when I was woken by Isaac's cell phone ringing.

Bodies slumbered all around me. I crept out, stepping over those who were sleeping. The sound of quiet snores and heavy breathing filled the room.

Isaac's low, urgent voice caused my pulse to race.

"Everything okay?" I asked as he hung up.

He nodded. "Yeah, that was Andrea. She's made contact with the other team leaders, and we need to convene. We're going to need to figure out what we're going to do with all the boys."

I chewed on my lower lip. "They won't be going back to the bases?"

"Not now that people know about them. You can imagine the field day the media will have with that—boy soldiers being trained underground. It would be a shit storm."

He was right.

"So, what's going to happen to them?"

His shoulders lifted in a shrug. "I'm not sure yet. That's why I need to meet with Andrea and whoever the leaders of the other bases are so we can come up with a plan about what happens next."

"You think everyone is going to get to stay together?" I asked anxiously.

"Honestly, love, probably not. I wish I could say we'll all live happily ever after, but chances are that's not going to happen."

My stomach churned. I wanted to grab him and cry 'but what about us,' but I knew this wasn't the time or place to have that conversation. My relationship with each of the guys meant the world to me, and at least when we'd had Hollan pushing us together and a job to do, I'd known we'd still be together as a unit. Now the future was a murky lake I could barely see into. I'd thought the base was going to be our home, but there'd be no chance of that happening now. We'd be inundated by the press, and be the target for anyone who wanted to cause us trouble.

"Do you want us to come with you?" I asked.

He shook his head, and my stomach sank. This was the start of it. The start of us all having to go our separate ways. "I'll have to take both vans to fit all the kids. I'll take a couple of the guys with me to switch shifts driving, but Alex is probably going to need to take Kingsley to the hospital to get his ribs X-rayed, so it'll most likely be Clay and Lorcan."

I didn't want any of them to go, but I didn't say so.

"Yeah, I should probably spend some time with my aunt anyway," I bluffed. "She really helped getting the boys out, and I've barely had a chance to see her."

Isaac nodded. He fixed me with his gaze, faint lines between his eyebrows, his lips pressed together as he looked down at me. "We'll come back, love."

I forced a smile. "Sure. I know that."

"Good. You're not getting rid of us that easily."

His words warmed my heart a little, but I still couldn't shake the coiling fear at my soul that I was losing them.

Chapter Twenty-two

They left that same day.

Both men and boys piled into the two vans taken from the base. Clay drove one, while Isaac drove the other, and Lorcan rode shotgun with Isaac, ready to take over the wheel whenever one of them needed a break.

I hugged and kissed each of the guys goodbye, holding back tears as I waved to the boys. Though I knew they'd return, I still felt as though they were taking a part of my heart with them.

Kingsley and Alex took the opportunity to leave to go to the hospital. I wanted to go with them, but it felt wrong to abandon my aunt to the chaos the house was currently in—pillows and blankets everywhere, together with piles of wet clothes, and a kitchen that looked as though a swarm of locusts had gone through it. Besides, there was nothing I could do to help at the hospital. I'd probably only get in the way. I'd be far more useful helping out here.

That didn't stop the tears from falling when I shut the door on them, though. My chest ached, and for a moment I just stood there, my forehead pressed against the back of the door.

Then I straightened and swiped away the tears with the back of my hand. They would be back. They promised. This wasn't the end.

Besides, I had stuff to do.

I set about picking up after all the people who'd spent the night here.

The house felt weirdly empty with them gone. It seemed strange to only be me and my aunt, knocking around in this big house. Just the two of us again, as though none of it had ever happened.

Aunt Sarah had been right. There was nothing to eat in this place. Everything even remotely edible had been cleared out by the boys. I needed to do some grocery shopping.

"I'm going to the store," I told Sarah. "You okay if I take your car?"

"Sure. I'm going to take a bath."

"Can I get you anything?"

"Just an entire kitchen full of food," she quipped.

I laughed. "I'll do my best."

At the store, I wandered around, dropping random things into the cart, completely lost in thought about everything that had happened. It seemed crazy to me that I didn't have my experiences scrawled onto my forehead, that everyone around me just carried on as normal. People walked past me, some saying hello, while others nodded and smiled their greeting. I wanted to grab them by the shoulders and spew out my story, but I doubted anyone would believe me, and I'd probably look like a mad woman.

Instead, I acted like a normal member of society, placing bread, milk, and cartons of juice into the cart.

I paid for the groceries and drove home again.

I climbed out of the car and, carrying as many grocery bags as possible, I made my way back into the house.

"Only me," I called as I walked in.

"Be down in a minute," came my aunt's muffled reply.

I used my shoulder to push open the kitchen door. Barging my way in, I turned and jumped out of my skin. Someone was sitting at the table. Gasping, I instinctively took a step back, the grocery bags falling from my arms. The carton of eggs spilled, several eggs cracking, clear albumen and yellow yolk leaking from the broken shell.

"Hello, Darcy."

Devlin!

"What are you doing here?" I managed. "How did you get in?"

"I'm a Ghost, remember, Darcy. I'm good at slipping into places without anyone noticing." He huffed air out through his nose in what I thought was supposed to be a poor imitation of a laugh. "Or at least, I *was* a Ghost, until you came along and ruined everything for me."

Ice water slipped through my veins. Seeing him here was not going to be a good thing. My thoughts went to the guys. I wasn't expecting Isaac and the others to be back for a few days, but Alex and Kingsley might return soon.

The ceiling above us creaked, and I suddenly remembered my aunt. If she knew something was wrong, she'd be able to call for help. But at the same time, I didn't want her to walk in on this.

"I didn't ruin anything." I edged back again. "You did that all by yourself by getting involved with Hollan."

He slammed his hand on the table, and I jumped and then froze. "I told you, that was a mistake!" His other hand remained beneath the table, and I flicked my line of sight down to it, trying to figure out what he was holding.

"Okay." My voice was small.

"Didn't you ever make a mistake?"

"I made plenty." *But they didn't get an innocent man killed,* I thought, but didn't say out loud.

I took another tiny step back, and he whipped a gun from beneath the table and pointed the muzzle directly at me. Automatically, I put both hands in the air, my heart lurching.

"If you'd just kept your mouth shut with that reporter," he snapped, "none of this would ever have happened."

I shook my head, my eyes wide. "I didn't know what that was at the time. I didn't know what my father told me even meant anything." This whole thing felt so unfair. So unjust. I'd never asked for any of this. "Besides, you could have just let it go. You didn't need to send Isaac and the others after me."

"Yes, I did. Or Hollan would have gotten the coordinates without me. You think that man ever intended on sharing? I should have known not to trust him—I knew it deep down in my gut. That was the whole reason I never told him the location of our base. Things would have been all right, but you messed everything up. You gave Hollan the co-ordinates, and now I'm finished because of you."

Footsteps creaked from above, and both of us looked up.

"Shooting me isn't going to solve anything." I wanted to keep the tremor from my voice, but it belied my true emotions and shook any-way.

His lip curled in a snarl. "Maybe not, but it'll sure as hell make me feel better."

"Darcy?" My aunt's voice filtered through the walls. "Who are you talking to?"

Devlin glared at me, daring me to say something.

"No one," I called back. "It's just the radio."

Apparently satisfied with my answer, he got to his feet, pushing the chair back behind him. The legs scraped across the floor with a screech that made me wince.

I glanced around, frantic, trying to see something I could use as a weapon. Was there anything in the grocery bags I'd dropped? The knife block was positioned on the countertop on the other side of the room. There wasn't much beside me, except the toaster and a chopping block, and I didn't think either of those was going to hold up much against a gun.

But I could sense my aunt making her way down from upstairs. After growing up in this house, I could track every creak and know exactly where the other person's feet were landing. She was getting closer, approaching the kitchen down the hallway, and I couldn't have her coming in here.

"Aunt Sarah, run!" I screamed. It was a pathetic attempt, but I'd had to do something. I grabbed the toaster from the counter and yanked, pulling the cord out of the wall, and threw it at Devlin. He lifted his arm to shield his face, but he moved too late and the item smacked him in the face.

I didn't wait to see how effective my attack had been. Instead, I ran for the back door, praying Sarah would have run for the front of the house. But as I reached the door and yanked on the handle, it didn't budge. Tears filled my eyes. Shit, it was locked. I stared for the key, frantically trying to spot it. There used to be one on the windowsill. But Devlin was already recovering, twisting to face me, swinging the gun around—

The kitchen door flung open, and before I knew what was happening, shots fired. I screamed, first as Devlin was hit in the gut by a bullet, and then again as he swung back around and fired in return.

I stared in horror as Aunt Sarah stood in the open doorway, brandishing a gun I hadn't seen before. But the gun wasn't the cause of my dismay. No, it was the circle of red that appeared on her chest, and the way she stared down at the wound in shock.

"Aunt Sarah!" My voice was a scream that would seem to echo through the house for months to come, like that of a ghost unable to rest.

My scream became a howl as she dropped to the floor, her hand against her chest. Bright red blood suddenly appeared between her slender fingers, and she glanced down, as though surprised at where it had come from. I rushed over and slid to the floor beside her. I lifted her head into my lap and then fumbled frantically for my phone. Where had I left it? My mind was a blur, but I knew I needed to call an ambulance.

"I have to call nine-one-one." I tried to rise, but her other hand caught my wrist.

"I'm sorry, Darcy."

"No, no." Her face blurred through my tears. "You don't have anything to be sorry for. I'm the one who should be sorry. I only ever caused you trouble."

She shook her head, but I could see she was weakening, her eyes slipping shut. "I'm sorry ... I'm not going to be around for you." Her voice broke, and her eyes rolled in her head.

Grief and fear ricocheted through me.

"No, you can't die! You can't. Just hold on. I'll get help." But her fingers around my wrist tightened, and it was enough to tell me that she didn't want me to leave her. She didn't want to die alone.

"No," I sobbed, not wanting to believe what was happening, wanting to push it all away, as though it was all a bad dream. "I love you, Aunt Sarah. Please don't go. Don't leave me. I love you so much, and I never told you enough. Please ..." I leaned over her, pressing my forehead against the hand covering the gunshot wound.

But her eyes slipped shut and a breath escaped her throat, long and rasping.

Her chest didn't rise again.

A scream of fury bubbled up inside me, and I gave voice to it, screeching my rage and grief, over and over. I snatched up the gun Sarah had been holding and went to where Devlin was lying on the floor. Teeth gritted, hatred and sorrow filling my soul in equal measures, I pointed the gun and squeezed the trigger, again, and again. *Bang, bang, bang.* His body jerked with each shot, until I'd emptied the clip into his body.

All the strength went from me, and I crumpled to the floor between the two dead bodies, and wailed my heartbroken grief helplessly into my hands.

Chapter Twenty-three

I wasn't completely sure what happened after.

Alex and Kingsley found me hunched over my aunt's body, but I couldn't have said how long I'd been kneeling there. I was barely aware of cops and flashing lights, and paramedics, and people asking me questions I was too numb to answer.

Words were thrown around like *break in* and *shooting*. I didn't know how much of this the guys would be able to make vanish, but right then I didn't care. I just wanted everything to go away, including myself.

When the police eventually gave up for the time being, perhaps seeing I was in shock, and promising to come back at a later date, I climbed the stairs to my aunt's room and curled up on her bed. The black hole that had appeared inside me when my father was shot had expanded, and it felt as though it would continue to expand until it swallowed me whole. I was utterly alone now. I had no one.

Over the next few days, Alex and Kingsley tried to talk to me, bringing me food that remained untouched, and drinks I barely managed sips of, and only because they practically forced me. I was unwashed and probably stank, but I didn't even care. I couldn't see any point in going on when everyone I ever cared about ended up dead. It was all so utterly pointless.

Isaac came back with Clay and Lorcan. I was sleeping and woke to him crouching beside the bed, looking at me in concern.

"Hey, love." His voice was softer than I'd ever heard before. "I'm so sorry about your aunt."

Something had been festering inside me since her death, and now Isaac was here, I could let it out.

"You could have killed him." They were the first words I'd spoken in days, and my voice came out as a raspy croak.

His eyebrows pulled together. "What?"

"You could have killed Devlin, but you cared for him, despite what he did. So he came after me, and he killed my aunt. This is your fault. My aunt dying is your fault."

Pain traversed his features. "No, love. That's not how it was at all."

I nodded. "Yes, it was. You had the chance to kill him, and you didn't. All I see when I look at any of you is that we all got my aunt killed. I'll never forgive myself for what I did, opening my mouth and starting this whole thing, and I'll never forgive you, either."

He shook his head. "You don't mean that."

"Yes, I do. I want you gone. You, Clay, Alex, Kingsley, and Lorcan. I don't want any part of this anymore. You need to go. Go and continue with whatever your jobs need you to do now. I'm no longer involved."

He stared at me, his green eyes filled with pain. "We're not just going to leave you."

"I said go!"

"You can't just check out on us, love. Not like this."

"Yes, I can. And if you don't go, I'll call the cops and tell them you're intruding. This isn't your house. I don't want you here. Any of you."

The words hurt to say. They cut me deep, slicing at my soul with every syllable. But I relished the pain. That was all I wanted to feel now. I deserved to hurt.

Abruptly, Isaac rose to his feet. "I'm going to get the others."

I rolled over in bed, facing the wall. "Don't bother."

I heard the swish of the bottom of the door against the carpet as it opened and closed, and then I was alone again, but not for long.

Kingsley came to me next, his deep voice, his weight depressing the mattress as he sat next to me. "This is grief, Darcy. It's normal to be feeling this way. You need to give yourself time."

"So give me time," I told him. "Leave me alone."

But they didn't.

One by one, they sat by my bedside, trying to get through to me, but I was dead inside.

Finally, they left me in peace, but only for long enough to allow me to get some sleep, and then they returned, continuing to try to coax me from the dark pit I'd sunk into.

Nothing worked.

I pushed them away, over and over again. I told them to leave me, I shouted at them, and screamed, and threw whatever I could get my hands on, which often ended up being the glasses of water or whatever plates of food they'd brought me. I started this whole thing as their prisoner in a cellar, with them providing me with what I needed to survive, and now the same thing was happening again, only this time I'd made myself the prisoner.

I lost track of the days. I either slept endlessly, or lay awake, staring at the walls or ceiling, floating through the vast black sea of my grief.

⁂

ONE MORNING, SOMETHING changed.

Out of my darkness, I noticed the light.

It was a shaft of hazy, early morning light, in a streak across my aunt's bed. It had landed on my bare toes and warmed my skin, and, instead of pulling my legs into my body and removing myself from its warmth, I stretched out farther and pushed more of my skin into the light.

The guys hadn't left me.

I was a mess. I had filthy hair, skin, and could barely remember the last time I'd brushed my teeth. I'd pushed them away and screamed at them and thrown things, and been the worst person imaginable, but still they'd remained.

I didn't know what had gone on in their lives since I'd checked out. I hadn't asked about the boys or any of the other bases, and for the first time since my aunt had died, I actually started to wonder. I started to care.

I was still staring at the shaft of light when the door opened and Clay walked in. He carried a plate with a couple of slices of toast, and in his other hand was a glass of juice. They'd stopped bringing me mugs of hot drinks when they realized how often I was going to throw them. Even though they'd done their best to clean up after me, the carpet would probably forever hold the stains from all those mugs of coffee.

He set the toast and juice onto the bedside table and cast me an anxious glance.

My lips twitched, and my gaze met his glance briefly, before shifting away. I was embarrassed. Embarrassed at how I looked and smelled, and embarrassed at how I'd behaved toward them.

He must have noticed the change in me, as, instead of hurrying out and hoping I didn't fling the toast at him, he stayed.

"How you feeling, sugar?"

I shrugged. "I ... I ..." My words caught like a tickle in the back of my throat during a situation where you weren't supposed to cough. "I'm not sure yet. How long has it been?"

"How long has—" he started to say, and then his sentence drifted off as he understood what I was asking. "Oh, you mean, how long has it been since ..."

He clearly didn't want to say the words, perhaps worrying that speaking out loud about my aunt dying would set me back again.

"Two weeks," he said instead. "Almost three."

"Three weeks?"

I could hardly believe it. It hadn't felt like that long, yet at the same time it had felt like a lifetime. I couldn't continue like this. I knew something had to change.

I glanced over at the juice and toast Clay had brought me and reached out for it. A flicker of a smile crossed his face, and he snatched the glass up for me, pushing it into my hands. Seeing how pleased he was that I was willingly going to eat and drink, a little ball of something I once recognized as happiness swelled inside my chest. And I realized I wanted to make him happy. It was such a small thing, but I'd connected to him again.

Alternating sips of orange juice between nibbles of the toast, I ate self-consciously, but without telling Clay to go away.

It was the first full meal I'd eaten in weeks, and I wasn't sure how my stomach was going to react to it.

"I'll go and tell the others you're feeling better." Clay put his hand on the sheets, above my thigh. "Everyone's been worried sick about you."

I glanced down at my hands. "Sorry," I said, my voice a hoarse whisper, my throat suddenly choked with tears again.

"Hey, no, it's okay." He took my hand and squeezed it tight. "We get it. We just care, that's all."

I nodded. "Thank you. Thank you for not giving up on me."

"We'd never give up on you, sugar. You must know that by now."

A tear slid down my cheek, and I nodded, not trusting myself to speak.

We sat like that for a moment, him perched on the edge of the bed, holding my hand, while I pulled myself together. Then he stood, and I knew he was going to get the others.

"Clay," I said, looking up at him, tears causing the room to shimmer. "Can you give me half an hour to shower and change? I feel disgusting."

I knew they'd all seen me like this numerous times, but for the first time I actually cared.

He nodded. "Of course. Anything else you need?"

I shook my head.

He smiled and leaned in and kissed the top of my head. "It's good to have you back, baby-doll. We've missed you."

And with that, he turned and left the room.

I climbed out of bed, my legs trembling. My aunt's bedroom had an adjoining bathroom, so I headed there, peeling off my filthy clothes as I went. I wrinkled my nose in disgust at myself, pinching the items between my thumb and finger and dropping them into a pile on the floor.

Naked, I reached in and turned on the shower. The water heated quickly, and steam began to fill the small space. I risked glancing down at my body. I'd lost a lot of weight in the last few weeks, my stomach concave, my hipbones showing, my thighs skinny, which, in turn, made my knees look too big. This wasn't a body I'd be showing off to the guys any time soon—not that sex was something I'd given any thought to lately.

I stood beneath the hot stream of water and lifted my face to the flow, allowing the water to wash away my tears and run through my hair. I used my aunt's products, the scent of them reminding me of her and making me cry all over again. She'd been more like a mother to me than an aunt, a mother I'd never truly appreciated, and now she was gone, I wished so hard I could go back and do things differently. I'd have given anything for one more hug, one more smile, one more conversation. But it didn't matter how much I wanted it, it was never going to happen.

Aunt Sarah was gone.

Chapter Twenty-four

I pulled myself together enough to dress in clean clothes and make my way downstairs.

Shyly, I pushed my way into the kitchen to find all the guys sitting around the table. This was the first time I'd been in here since everything had happened, and I couldn't help picture the bodies in the same spots as I'd left them.

Isaac must have read my thoughts, as he got to his feet. "Come on, let's go to the living room."

He stopped in front of me then wrapped his arms around me and pulled me against his chest. I bunched my fists in his shirt and let him hold me, even as silent tears dampened the material.

He released me only for Alex to step in, squeezing me hard and kissing the top of my head.

Then Lorcan, cupping my face in his hands, his fingers lacing in the damp strands of my hair. He lowered his forehead to mine, noses touching, and then placed the lightest of kisses on the corner of my mouth. "We've missed you," he told me. I smiled at him in return.

He moved out of the way to allow Kingsley to scoop me up in a bear hug, surrounding me with his big body, making me feel safe. "How are your ribs?" I asked him, standing on tiptoes, my face pressed against his shoulder.

"Better," he replied. "No more pain."

"That's good."

He released me, and together we all went into the living room, selecting spots on the couch and the chair.

"Tell me," I said, "what's happened to everyone?"

Isaac answered my question. "It's gone, love. The whole place is finished. A new home is being created for the boys, but they won't be trained to work undercover. They'll go on to live normal lives. They may not be perfect lives, but they'll be safe."

His words confused me. "Gone? What do you mean, gone?"

"The locations of the bases are compromised. What remains of the bases is being broken down. The equipment will be either destroyed, or wiped, and moved on. Everyone is being reassigned."

I looked up at them, blinking through my tears. "Everyone?"

He nodded. "Yes, even us."

My heart grew cold in my chest, the little bit of hope and relief I'd experienced upon waking threatening to crust over again. So I was going to lose them, too. "Reassigned to where? Doing what?"

"That depends."

I frowned, still not understanding. "On what?"

"On you, Darcy."

I looked around at their solemn faces, faces I'd grown to love, and my heart threatened to crack. I wasn't sure how much more pain I could take. Over the past few weeks, I'd managed to convince myself that I could hunker down and pretend none of the past month had ever happened. But I knew I'd never be able to pretend they weren't a part of me now. Since my aunt died, all I'd experienced was a deep sense of emptiness, like my organs had been scooped from my body, and I was like one of those porcelain dolls, hollow on the inside. I hadn't wanted to think about trying to get through each day. Just getting through an hour had felt like a monumental task. I'd been all alone in the world, and I'd felt it so acutely it was like a void existed around me, or like I was the castle in the middle of a moat, and I had no way of lowering the drawbridge.

But they'd been my drawbridge.

And now I was terrified they were about to pull it away again.

"I don't understand."

Isaac covered the back of my hand with his. "Jobs can be found for us here in D.C., love. They won't be the same caliber as what we were working before, but we still have some skills the government will find useful." He allowed himself the faintest smile.

"You mean you're coming to work, here in the city?"

I looked around at their faces.

Alex nodded. "I can work at the hospital, no problem. It's already being arranged."

Lorcan lifted his hand. "Security for me—the Pentagon always needs people they can trust."

"And I'll be dealing with cyber security," Isaac said.

"I'll be working with the FBI, helping to counsel agents who've dealt with violence in the field," Kingsley said.

"And you, Clay?" I looked to him.

He shrugged. "Actually, I'm taking the opportunity to get out of government stuff for awhile. I'm planning on setting up shop, specialize in motorcycles, maybe. Something a little more laidback."

I stared between them all, fresh tears threatening to fill my eyes, but this time tears of happiness. "So, you're all staying?"

Isaac grinned. "Yeah, we're staying. Assuming you'll have us?"

With his words, my broken heart grew tendrils and began to entwine with each other inside my chest. They hadn't given up on me, even after everything. And even through all the pain and violence, love still existed inside me.

"But you'll all be apart." My voice cracked.

I hated the thought of them all separated. They'd been a team since they were children, and they did everything together. I couldn't imagine them all going their separate ways and only meeting up occasionally to share a beer and watch a game.

"No, we won't."

They moved to close around me, Isaac holding one hand, Alex the other. Clay stood behind me, his hand on my shoulder, while Lorcan crouched on the rug in front of me. Kingsley took up a spot on the arm of the couch. It was as though they all wanted to be near me in the same way I always wanted to be around them. We worked this way. I didn't know why, and I knew it wasn't exactly a traditional setup, but we were happy when we were together.

"What are you saying?" I dared to ask.

Isaac continued. "That we'll see each other every night. We'll see each other every morning. We'll be here to fight about what we watch on the television, and over who took out the trash."

"Will that be enough for you, Darcy?" Kingsley asked. "Without all the madness and secrets and underground bunkers. Will it be enough to just have us in your life?"

"Just you?" I almost laughed over the words, a giddy kind of laughter. "There can never be a *just* you. Not with the five of you. I'd have been lucky to have any one of you singly, but to have all of you together? How could that ever possibly not be enough?"

They glanced at each other, smiling.

"But what about me?" I asked, suddenly panicked. "Am I going to be enough for all of you? I mean, we haven't exactly had a normal setup, but now we will. How will you all feel with only me?"

"You're crazy," Clay laughed. "We love you, sugar, all of us do. And we've grown up sharing the things we love our whole lives. It would almost be strange to do something any other way. But you get to call the shots, okay? One of us, two of us, or all of us, or hell, if you're sick to death of us all and you want us to leave you the hell alone for the night, then we get that, and that's fine, too."

I hid a small smile. "I don't think I'd ever want you guys to leave me alone." Warmth flared in my cheeks.

Alex squeezed my hand. "Well, that's good to know, too."

I could barely believe what I was hearing. This was what they wanted? To be with me?

"So you guys are all going to move in here, with me, into this house? Permanently?"

"We'd like to, love," Isaac said.

Clay pushed his hand through his hair. "But only if you want us to. No pressure."

A sob of happiness swelled inside my chest then rose like a balloon, threatening to burst from between my lips. I clamped my hand over my mouth to hold it back, and nodded.

"Is that a yes?" Alex asked.

Clay looked to him. "Was that a yes?"

Lorcan seemed equally confused by my reaction. "Is she going to have us?"

"It's a yes," I burst. "Of course it's a yes. I could never imagine my life without you all in it."

The guys grinned at each other. Clay punched Lorcan in the shoulder. Kingsley threw me a wink.

Isaac leaned in and kissed me.

"Then that's a deal."

One Month Later

"**H**oney, I'm home!"

I grinned as the call came through the house, the front door opening. It was an ongoing joke between us, each of the guys calling the same thing as they stepped through the door every evening. I'd grown to love the sound.

Each of them came up behind me when they returned, as I was normally found in the kitchen, making food for us. Even with my back to them, I could tell who it was, not only from their voice or the way they walked, but from the way they kissed me from behind.

Lorcan would hook one arm across the front of my body and kiss the side of my neck. Alex liked to grab me by the waist and pull me to him from behind. Kingsley would wrap his arms around me fully, holding me tight as he leaned in to kiss me. Isaac wouldn't even touch me, but would sweep the hair from my neck and then pepper soft kisses down to my nape, making me shiver.

I knew this was Clay, however, could smell the engine oil on his clothing the moment he walked in. Plus, the others were already home.

He grabbed my waist, tickling me to make me squeal. I knew he liked the way the tickling made me fold in half, pushing my bottom out toward him, which he gave a playful spank.

"Hey, baby," he said.

"Hey, yourself." I twisted in his arms for a proper kiss. His mouth claimed mine, and I pressed my body up against his, not caring if I covered my clothes in oil. He smelled good, all manly and sexy.

I heard the swoosh of the kitchen door opening.

"Put her down. It's my turn."

Isaac. I was always shyer with him. Unlike the others, he was the only one I hadn't had some kind of sex with, though I knew it was coming. It was important that we were all on an even keel.

We hadn't broached sex since my aunt had died. Plenty of affection, yes, but not full sex. After the weeks in bed, both my body and my heart had needed time to recover. I knew it must have been frustrating for them, though none of them ever pushed me, but I needed to make sure I was ready.

Clay chuckled and spun me around to face Isaac, but he stayed close, so I was sandwiched between the two of them.

Isaac stepped in and kissed me, too, his fingers spanning my throat and jaw. His lips teased mine, his tongue darting into my mouth as he kissed me slow and deep, turning me to putty in his hands.

"Now, this looks fun," came a voice from the door.

The others had come to find us, perhaps wondering what we were up to. I stopped kissing Isaac long enough to peep around him and see them watching, Alex and Lorcan with identical, knowing smiles on their faces. Kingsley stood right behind them, and his eyes darkened with barely veiled lust as he saw me sandwiched between Clay and Isaac.

I kissed Isaac again, pressing myself into him, knowing I was putting on a show now the others were here. Clay stepped in closer, his hands on my hips, tracing the curves of my body. He swept my hair away from my nape and placed his lips to that spot. As he nudged his hips forward, I could already feel that he wanted me. Nerves fluttered inside me, but they were excited nerves. I liked the feel of them watching. It was undoubtedly sexy.

I'd set the table for dinner, but Isaac didn't seem to care. He lifted me, my thighs wrapping around his hips, and pulled me away from Clay, spinning me around. My bottom hit the wood of the table, and a number of items behind me toppled over. Clay stepped forward and swept the knives, forks, and placemats out of the way. Then his hands supported my shoulders as Isaac reclined me across the wood, as though I was a precious object that might shatter if dropped too roughly.

My breath grew tight in my lungs in anticipation.

The others moved in closer, their eyes all fixed on me. I'd never felt like I was under such focus before, and my nipples tightened in response, crinkling under the lace of my bra. My lips tingled from their kisses, every inch of my skin sensitized and begging to be touched. I felt like a delicious dish spread out across the table, waiting to be devoured.

Clay's hands reached to the buttons of my shirt, popping them open, one by one. Isaac remained between my legs, his fingers working the button on my jeans. I knew they were going to get me naked, and I wasn't going to protest for a second.

Another set of hands—Lorcan's this time—pulled the shirt from my left shoulder, while Clay worked the right. I lifted up slightly, allowing Lorcan to pull the item of clothing from beneath me. Isaac took a step back, giving himself space to pull the jeans from my hips, leaving me in only my underwear.

Numerous hands and eyes roved across my body. The men surrounded me like I was a sacrifice, and I drew a breath, subconsciously sucking in my stomach and arching my back to push out my tits.

Between my thighs, Isaac dropped to his knees, bringing his face level with my pussy. I was still wearing my panties, but they were already wet and clinging to my folds. He leaned in, his nose nudging my clit, and then he ran his tongue across the material, from the base of me, right up to my mound. I gasped and squirmed on the table, but I had Clay and Lorcan at each shoulder, keeping me flat. Clay leaned over and kissed me first, his hand cupping the back of my head for support, then Lorcan nibbled my shoulder and up to my neck. Hands were on the straps of my bra, tugging them down, followed by the cups, to reveal my breasts, the nipples hard.

I allowed myself a peek at the others. Kingsley and Alex were both watching. Alex's hand was at the front of his pants, rubbing his erection over the material, waiting his turn. It wouldn't be long. I wanted them all.

The whisper of a breath crossed my skin, goose bumps puckering in response. A hot mouth covered my nipple, and I looked down to see the top of Lorcan's dark hair. Reaching down, I laced my fingers through the silky strands. His teeth grated the hard peak, pulling it fully into his mouth, sending sparks of pleasure down into my core.

Between my thighs, Isaac pulled my panties to one side, and then nudged my legs even farther apart. Then his mouth was on me fully, and his tongue speared inside me, pushing between my folds. I gasped, my back arching from the table. Fuck, that felt so good. Clay continued to kiss my mouth, his tongue dancing with mine, while Lorcan suckled my nipple. I was in a halo of pleasure, barely knowing where to focus, my mind spinning with all the sensations battling for attention.

A large hand made contact with my thigh, and I looked over enough to see Kingsley standing beside Clay. He traced the curve of my body, lingering over my other breast. His finger circled my nipple, and the areola tightened, then he traced down, running over my ribs and the dip of my stomach. His touch skimmed my hip and down the side, eventually slipping beneath me, his large palm cupping my bottom. I was already soaked, and I knew he'd be able to feel where my natural lubricant had dripped down from my slit, between the crack of my ass. The scent of my arousal filled the air. His finger traced the crease between my cheeks until he reached what he wanted.

He circled the tight pucker of my ass, using the lubrication from my pussy and Isaac's saliva.

"Relax, baby," he growled in his deep timbre, before pushing just the tip inside my ass.

I mewled, almost lifting off the table. Kingsley continued to finger me, my entire rear end held by his big palm, that sensation alone making me crazy, especially with how he looked down at me while he did it. Isaac licking my pussy over my panties caused the sensations to combine, almost sending me out of my mind.

"Take off your clothes," I gasped, addressing them all. "I want you all naked, too."

Though Isaac stayed between my thighs, ignoring my request, the other men released their hold on me. They tugged off their clothing, pulling off shirts and removing pants. Freeing their erections. I didn't know where to look first, each of them so beautiful in their own way—Clay, tan and blond. Lorcan, dark and tattooed. Alex, tall and slender, and Kingsley thick with muscle. I was surrounded by different male bodies, each of them perfect in their own way. They ran their hands down the lengths of their cocks, never taking their eyes off me as they masturbated.

I wasn't worried about us needing to be safe. After we'd talked about the nature of our relationship, Alex had stepped into action, making sure each of us came up clean in tests, and then getting me on a long-term contraceptive. I wanted to think children were in our future one day, but I was still young, and it was important we learned how to live as a family by ourselves first. That wasn't to say I didn't dream about it, though, and I noticed each time one of them made a comment about kids running around here one day, or what names they liked, or if they'd prefer to have a boy or a girl.

Isaac pulled his mouth from me and got to his feet. He hooked his fingers down either side of my panties and rolled them down my thighs. He plucked the underwear from the tips of my toes and then grinned. "I'm going to keep these for later, love," he said with a smirk. "I think I should have a keepsake for our first time together."

I pushed him playfully in the stomach with my foot, and he rolled up the underwear and put them in his back pocket before his hands went to his shirt. I lay there before him, with my legs spread as he slowly undressed himself, but I wasn't left wanting for long. Lorcan slid his hand down across my stomach and then through the little patch of blonde curls.

"Fuck, you're so wet," he groaned.

"She's wet for me first," Isaac reminded him. "You can take her when she's even wetter."

His words made me moan, and I almost came then and there, the moment Lorcan's fingers pushed inside me. He hooked them forward, so the tips pressed against my g-spot, and a cry escaped my throat. Christ, this was the hottest thing I'd ever done in my life, and this *was* my life now. This wasn't going to be a one-time thing. These were my guys, and they could take me over and over, as many times as they liked, in whatever order they liked, time and time again.

Isaac pushed Lorcan's hand out of the way, and Lorcan looked me in the eye as he brought his fingers to his mouth and sucked them off, one by one.

"You taste as sweet as you look," he said.

"My turn," Alex said, stepping forward. His fingers slid over my flat belly, but instead of pushing inside me, he stopped at the bundle of nerves right above my slit and strummed. The effect was instantaneous, and my whole body tensed in response, coiled with the building pleasure.

But my focus turned to Isaac as he stood naked between my thighs, his cock held in one hand, his other hand placed on my thigh. I caught the glimpse of his dragon tattoo curling over his shoulder. He stepped forward, his cockhead pressing against my spread slit.

He smoldered down at me. "Oh, love, you have no idea how long I've wanted to be inside you."

With those words, he pushed inside me, sliding long and deep. He grabbed my hips as he slammed into me, pulling out before driving in, faster and deeper. My arousal built with every stroke, and my breasts bounced with the movement and my gasps for breath.

Alex continued to work my clit, his gaze flicking between my face and my pussy. His cock jutted out toward me, and I reached for him, circling my fingers around him. He was hard and hot, and I pumped him while he rubbed my clit. The other men's hands were still all over me, Clay now feasting on my tits, while Lorcan sucked my cream from his fingers. But it was Isaac who kept eye contact with me, his gaze dark and intense, almost angry, as he pumped into me.

My inner walls started to convulse around his cock, gripping his length. "Oh, God, Isaac. I'm coming."

I couldn't concentrate on more than one guy in that moment, and I released my hold on Alex's cock.

My orgasm hit me hard and fast, my whole body bucking with its force. Though I'd locked gazes with Isaac the whole time, now I couldn't help squeezing my eyes shut, needing to block everything off from view as pleasure took hold of all my senses.

Alex removed his fingers from my clit. He must have sensed I was too sensitive there now to be touched.

Isaac gave me a moment to allow the final sparks of my climax to shudder through me, but then he started up again, fucking me harder. His hips slammed against mine, bruising. I watched his face, normally so controlled and together, screw up as he lost it. He groaned long and hard as he came inside me, holding himself deep, his body eclipsing mine.

Isaac came down from his orgasm, breathing hard, and the other guys moved enough to allow him to kiss me. I wrapped my arms around his neck, the kiss no longer erotic, but still sensual.

He leaned in, his mouth against my ear. "Thanks, love."

I smiled at him. "Thanks, yourself."

"Back off, Isaac," Kingsley said, though his tone was teasing. "Let someone else through."

I caught Kingsley's eye, and he reached out and took my hand, pulling me to sitting. He dropped to one of the kitchen chairs and tugged me off the table and onto his lap to straddle him. I was soaked now, still filled with Isaac's cum, but Kingsley didn't seem to care. I remembered how big he was, how, when we'd first had sex, I wasn't sure he'd even fit. But now I was already wet and stretched, and when he pulled me onto him, I settled myself right over his erection and sank down deep.

"Oh, fuck."

His finger went back to my ass, and he edged the digit inside me, using the slipperiness of our fluids. It burned a little, but I was already too high to care, and that pain quickly morphed into pleasure as he pushed in up to his knuckle. I knew what he was doing, stretching me to be ready for one of the other guys. I didn't know who, and the idea both excited and aroused me, though I wasn't without my nerves. But I wanted all of them, in every way possible. I wanted my body to be theirs.

Kingsley's finger sank as deep as his cock. He was so big, both his fingers and his dick, and I knew I wasn't going to last long. I glanced down into the space between us, loving how our skin contrasted. I arched my back, leaning forward to see how his thick cock stretched my folds, the creaminess of my arousal coating his dick.

We kissed, frantic gasps and nibbles, and out of the corner of my eye, I could see the remaining three standing there, cocks in hand, watching the action.

Kingsley's movements were rough and raw, his hips bucking up into mine, his finger pumping into me with every thrust of his cock. I'd barely come down from my previous orgasm, and already I could feel myself almost on the edge, my inner muscles pulsating around him. My fingers gripped his shoulders for balance, and my hold increased the closer my second orgasm got, my nails digging into his skin. The combination of being penetrated in two places meant it was coming harder and faster than before.

"Oh, fuck, Kingsley," I cried, as my body bucked and writhed on his. I couldn't kiss him, couldn't think, a slave to the pleasure wracking through me.

Kingsley responded to my climax and came as well, his hips pistoning into mine. I blinked through bleary eyes, watching his teeth clench, and feeling his cock swell. His free hand clutched my hip hard, pushing me onto him as he emptied himself inside me.

I was full now, wet and dripping, but it was far from over. Clay caught my hand and pulled me off Kingsley and onto the floor, so I was on my hands and knees. I knew what he wanted and opened my mouth willingly for him. He fed me his cock, the taste of musk and salt, mixed with the faintest engine oil from his new job, coating my tongue.

But to my surprise, he backed off, and his dick slipped from between my lips. Clay shook his head and pulled me to my feet. He touched my cheek and kissed me. "No, let's go upstairs. You're too good for the floor."

He reached beneath my thighs and lifted me up in much the same way Isaac had done when he'd put me on the table. His erection pressed between our stomachs, and he kissed me again. I thrust my tongue into his mouth, getting a little thrill from the idea that he could taste himself on me, just as I'd tasted myself on Isaac's tongue.

We moved as a unit, Isaac leading the way to open doors, while Clay carried me. I felt like an Egyptian princess, lifted high for the men to worship.

Before I'd barely realized we'd mounted the stairs, we were already in my bedroom.

Clay kissed me again before placing me on the bed. Then he gave my ass a playful smack. "I want you on your hands and knees again. But this time on the bed."

I did as he instructed, getting to all four, while the men all stood around me. Clay was the first to move, positioning himself so his thighs pressed against the side of the bed, bringing his dick to mouth level.

On the other side of the bed, Lorcan reached to my nightstand and opened to drawer. It didn't take much rummaging before he found what he needed.

I cocked my eyebrows. "You knew I had lube in my bedside drawer?"

He gave me a dangerous smile. "Doesn't every woman have lube in her bedside drawer?"

He surprised a laugh from me. "I have no idea!" But I *did* know what he wanted the lube for.

"Look at me, sugar," said Clay, and so I did.

Movement came behind me, weight depressing the mattress as someone climbed on with me, and I knew it was Lorcan. "I want to take your ass, princess. It's fucking gorgeous. You think you can handle me?"

I sucked in a breath, but nodded. "Yeah, I can handle you."

Clay's fingers touched beneath my chin, lifting my gaze to his. He focused me in his stormy eyes. "Just relax, sugar. Breathe and look at me. This will feel good, I promise. None of us would ever hurt you. Ever."

I nodded, believing him, trusting him.

I glanced back over my shoulder to see Lorcan positioned behind me. He squirted out a good dollop of lube, and I hissed air in over my teeth as he applied it to my hole.

"Cold," I said, and I heard him chuckle.

I smiled as well, but the smile faded as he worked the lube into my ass, and then down his dick. His fingers were working magic, and I closed my eyes to focus on the sensation. It wasn't painful, not yet. Kingsley had already stretched me.

"Look up at me," Clay said.

Lorcan's fingers vanished from my ass, and were replaced by the smooth head of his cock. I felt the tension as he pushed, and I instinctively tensed.

"Breathe," Clay told me again, his thumb stroking my jaw. "Take him for me. Take him for all of us."

"Ah, fuck," I heard Alex gasp, and I glanced over to see him masturbating over us, his gaze fixed on the scene before him. I wanted him, too, but first I had to take Lorcan.

Lorcan pushed his hips forward, and he slid deeper, breaching my tight ring. I sucked in another breath, and he stilled, allowing me to get used to the stretch.

I kept Clay's gaze even as he pushed the head of his dick toward my mouth again. I parted my lips for him, letting him slide his cock back over my tongue. Though the feel of Lorcan's cock in my ass battled for my attention, I wanted to make it good for Clay. I loosened my jaw farther, taking him as deep as I could. Bobbing my head back and forth, I deep-throated him. I barely kept my balance as I lifted one hand on the mattress to cup his balls, my finger tracing along the smooth base of his perineum. His cock jerked in my mouth as I ran my lips up and down the steely length of him, taking him deeper each time.

"Damn, sugar," Clay gasped from above me, his voice strangled. "You have no fucking idea how hot this is."

I thought I probably did, but my mouth was too full to reply.

"Ah, fuck," he groaned before coming hard, jetting streams down my throat.

With salty nectar filling my senses, I swallowed what I could, some dripping from the sides of my mouth.

I gave him a final lick, his erection already growing soft, before I let him slide from between my lips.

"Jesus Christ," Clay said, his breath ragged. "That was the best fucking blow job of my life."

With Clay taken care of, and Lorcan still held inside me, I looked to the remaining member of our group.

"Alex." I reached for him.

I still had Lorcan behind me, but I wanted them both. I straightened to my knees, while Alex dropped to his in front of me. His cock was longer than the others, sticking out from the thatch of blond curls at the juncture of his thighs.

He touched my cheek. "I don't want to hurt you."

I shook my head. "Never."

My Alex, the one who always took care of me. We kissed, and he showed no repulsion, though he must have tasted Clay's cum on my tongue. Lorcan held himself still behind me, though it must have taken him an insane amount of self control not to pound my ass until he came.

Alex kneeled lower, and I edged forward, bringing Lorcan with me, and then settled my knees on the outside of Alex's. I took hold of his cock and pressed it to my slit, and he lifted his hips, sliding between my folds. I'd never been so wet, filled with cum and my own cream, making his passage easy. In this position he wouldn't be able to drive deep, but, with Lorcan already taking up space, I thought it might be all I could handle. Besides, the position put pressure directly on my sensitized clit, and as the two men started to move inside me, awkwardly at first, but then creating a rhythm all their own, I felt my third orgasm for the evening already on the brink. I'd been close as soon as Lorcan had penetrated me, but had managed to hold off. Now, I was pressed between their beautiful bodies, with the taste of Clay still on my tongue, and one of them thrusting into me from behind, and one in front, and with Isaac, Clay, and Kingsley all watching the show, having already come themselves.

Was this why women were capable of multiple orgasms? Was it so we could take this many men and continue to experience pleasure, over and over, with every one of them?

Lorcan came first, his steely self-control giving way with a roar. I knew he was holding himself back, not wanting to hurt me, but he'd given me plenty of time for my body to get used to him. I reached back to clutch his thigh, urging him on as his dick slid in and out of my ass, the lube easing the way.

"Fuck, Princess. You're so fucking tight. I'm gonna come."

He pulled out of me at the exact moment he gave way to his orgasm and hot cum splattered over my ass cheeks and lower back. He paused, panting hard, his head bent so he pressed his forehead to my shoulder.

I still had Alex inside me, and I turned my attention to him now. Now it was just the two of us, we collapsed to the bed, kissing hard. I was sore and swollen, and Alex must have sensed it. He flipped me onto my back, and then, kneeling between my thighs, lifted one of my feet to hook over his shoulder. He fucked me, slowly and sensually, and the sound of my wetness filled the room, though it didn't embarrass me. They'd all contributed, all the men now watching the final climax. They moved near to me on the bed, Clay knotting his fingers in my hair, Isaac lowering his mouth to my nipple. Kingsley reached between my thighs to strum my clit, and Lorcan kissed my lips.

Alex's movements grew faster, and with it so did Kingsley's finger on my clit. They were going to wring another climax from me, and I was powerless to fight against it.

My final orgasm for the night clutched me in its grasp, and I cried out. My mind spun, my toes curling as it powered through me again and again. My pussy pulsed and Alex came, shooting his seed inside me. He held himself deep for a moment, and then pulled out, leaving me a quivering, shaking mess. I gasped for breath, my chest lifting and falling. My whole body ached, and I knew I'd feel it in the morning, but I didn't care. How could I want for anything else after my body had been consumed by these five sexy men? They each held me, touched me, tasted me. They were all I needed, and it seemed, somehow miraculously, I was all they needed, too. We'd been through so much together, but this was us now. We were happy, the six of us.

Together.

They kissed me, one by one, each finding a part of my body to fit against, resting a head on my belly, or beside my shoulder, or pulling my foot over their laps. I looked around at us, and my heart swelled with a crazy kind of happiness.

I grinned across at them.

"I think we're going to need a bigger bed."

THE END

LOVED WHAT YOU'VE READ? Make sure you sign up to my Reverse Harem newsletter! I'll have a new series starting this spring – a fantasy series called 'Chronicles of the Four' – so if you want to stay up to date about the release, make sure you sign up! https://landing.mailerlite.com/webforms/landing/e2x3e1

And if you enjoyed this book, or any of the others in the series, I'd love it if you took a moment to write a quick review. It only needs to be a line or two, just saying what you did or didn't like. Getting reviews can make or break a series, and give the author a boost to write you more books! Thank you!

About the Author

Marissa Farrar has always been in love with being in love. But since she's been married for numerous years and has three young daughters, she's conducted her love affairs with multiple gorgeous men of the fictional persuasion.

The author of thirty novels, she has been a full time author for the last six years. She predominantly writes paranormal romance and urban fantasy, but has branched into contemporary fiction as well.

If you want to know more about Marissa, then please visit her website at www.marissa-farrar.blogspot.com. You can also find her at her facebook page, www.facebook.com/marissa.farrar.author or follow her on twitter @marissafarrar.

She loves to hear from readers and can be emailed at marissafarrar@hotmail.co.uk and to stay updated on all her new Reverse Harem books, just sign up to her newsletter! https://landing.mailerlite.com/webforms/landing/e2x3e1

Also by the Author

The Monster Trilogy:
Defaced
Denied
Delivered

The Spirit Shifters Series:
Autumn's Blood
Saving Autumn
Autumn Rising
Autumn's War
Avenging Autumn
Autumn's End

The Serenity Series:
Alone
Buried
Captured
Dominion
Endless

The Dhampyre Chronicles:
Twisted Dreams

Twisted Magic

The Flux Series
Flux
After Flux

The Blood Courtesans Vampire Romance:
Stolen

Contemporary Fiction Novels
The Second Chances
Dirty Shots
Cut Too Deep
Survivor
The Sound of Crickets

Dark Fantasy/horror novels:
Underlife
The Dark Road

Printed in Great Britain
by Amazon